PM9 CONTENTS

Explore the world of digest magazines.

Pulp Modern

Vol. 2 No. 9 Fall 2022

Brandon Barrows

Ramsey Campbell

Sarah Cannavo

John Kojak

Anthony Perconti

M.E. Proctor

Stanley Rutgers

Wendy Velasquez

Lisa Voorhees

Edited by Alec Cizak
Uncle B. Publications, LLC

Pulp Modern Vol. 2 No. 9 Fall 2022
Published and produced by
Uncle B. Publications, LLC and Larque Press LLC
Pulp Modern is funded in part by Yuan Sang.

Opinions expressed belong to their individual authors.

Chief Editor: Alec Cizak
Design: Richard Krauss
Cover, Title Page, Contents Page, and Editorial artwork: Allen K
Interior Illustrations: Darren Auck, Theo Ellsworth, Brad W. Foster, Allen K,
Rick McCollum, and Michael Neno.
Cartoons: Bob Vojtko, reprinted from *Fishtales for Supper* No. 1.

Printed on demand from October 2022
Printed in the United States of America and other countries.

Contact information for Uncle B. Publications, LLC may be obtained through
the website: pulpmodern.net
Contact information for Larque Press LLC may be obtained through the
website: larquepress.com

All stories herein are works of fiction. All of the characters, organizations,
and events portrayed in this journal are either products of the authors'
imaginations or are used fictitiously.

ISBN-978-1-957034-16-4

ALLEN K. '22

From the Editor

Alec Cizak

Many conjecture the appeal of horror. The more affluent a society gets, the more it likes to *study* things. When something is studied, whatever appeal it once had can be lost. This happened to me briefly with movies in general when I studied film theory as an undergrad in the early 1990s. Yuppies who'd never been in the back of a cab, let alone actually driven one for a living, relentlessly psychoanalyzed my favorite flick of all time, *Taxi Driver*. I *had* driven a cab for a living. I understood Travis Bickle's loneliness better than anyone in that classroom. Especially the professor, who began each semester apologizing for having been born with testicles. I offered several objections to the snooty dismissals of Travis Bickle's concerns, always greeted with the same derision know-nothing snobs spew at anyone who exposes them to a life experience that collides with what the media tells them to believe. By the end of my third film theory class, I despised cinema. Film theory robbed me of the joy I once felt while watching a great movie. It took me years to regain that love. The same holds true for those who would analyze horror. Look too deeply into the abyss, you may find no abyss at all. And that's worse than not knowing.

Horror works best when it's unexplained. It takes someone with college degrees a long time to figure this out. Trust me. I used to be one of these goofballs attempting to extract profound meaning from gothic literature. A high school teacher once laughed at me for suggesting "The Fall of the House of Usher" is about incest. She told me to get my mind out of the gutter and just enjoy the story. And while most would argue Usher *is* about incest, that teacher was, essentially correct (I learned she passed away earlier this year; May she rest in peace). Sometimes you got to put down the notebook and pick up a box of popcorn.

And relax.

Practitioners of horror from the 1970s and 1980s would probably agree. That's why the 70s and 80s gave us horror's high point. There might be some throwaway explanation for that glob of bubblegum absorbing every living human it makes contact with, but that's not the horror of the situation. The horror of the situation is the *situation itself*. If one is being chased by a homicidal maniac wielding a knife or chainsaw or something even more creatively destructive, one will not stop to psychoanalyze the killer and perhaps engage the killer in a discussion of childhood trauma. Horror is the *moment* one's life is threatened. Such horror can be immediate. Or it can be a slow burn. A town, city, state, or country gradually being taken over by an irrational alien lifeforce can prolong that moment of horror as protagonists wonder when it will be *their* turn to have *their* minds corrupted. Or when the aliens will decide to simply kill those who don't go along with their grand plan.

I bring all this up because this month's *Pulp Modern* is focused entirely on the weird and horrific. In constant effort to move this digest closer to its natural, pulpy roots, I chose stories this time around that didn't dwell on the why, only the what. What is the horror? What is the threat? And how will the protagonist(s) survive? *Will* the protagonist(s) survive? One of the refreshing aspects of the horror genre is that happy endings are not required. Those who would dismiss horror for not being realistic miss its fundamental privilege: Horror is allowed to reflect the ultimate tragedy of life—that it is finite. That all your dreams and aspirations will one day amount to nothing. At least, as far as *you're* concerned.

Enjoy!

Alec Cizak
Editor

*He had never noticed
how strongly the house
smelled of old books,
nor how unpleasant the
smell could be.*

Out of Copyright

Ramsey Campbell

The widow gazed wistfully at the pile of books. "I thought they might be worth something."

"Oh, some are," Tharne said. "That one, for instance, will fetch a few pence. But I'm afraid your husband collected books indiscriminately. Much of this stuff isn't worth the paper it's printed on. Look, I'll tell you what I'll do—I'll take the whole lot off your hands and give you the best price I can."

When he'd counted out the notes, the wad over his heart was scarcely reduced. He carried the bulging cartons of books to his van, down three gloomy flights of stairs, along the stone path which hid beneath lolling grass, between gateposts whose stone globes grew continents of moss. By the third descent he was panting. Nevertheless he grinned as he kicked grass aside; the visit had been worthwhile, certainly.

He drove out of the cracked and overgrown streets, past rusty cars laid open for surgery, old men propped on front steps to wither in the sun, prams left outside houses as though in the hope that a thief might adopt the baby. Sunlight leaping from windows and broken glass lanced his eyes. Heat made the streets and his perceptions waver. Glimpsed in the mirror or sensed looming at his back, the cartons resembled someone crouching behind him. They smelled dustier than the streets.

Soon he reached the crescent. The tall Georgian houses shone white. Beneath them the van looked cheap, a tin toy littering the street. Still, it wasn't advisable to seem too wealthy when buying books. He dumped the cartons in his hall, beside the elegant curve of the staircase. His secretary came to the door of her office. "Any luck?"

"Yes indeed. Some first editions and a lot of rare material. The man knew what he was collecting."

"Your mail came," she said in a tone which might have announced the police. This annoyed him: he prided himself on his legal knowledge, he observed the law scrupulously. "Well, well," he demanded, "who's saying what?"

"It's that American agent again. He says you have a moral obligation to pay Lewis's widow for those three stories. Otherwise, he says—let's see—'I shall have to seriously consider recommending my clients to boycott your anthologies.' "

"He says that, does he? The bastard. They'd be better off boycotting him." Tharne's face grew hot and swollen; he could hardly control his grin. "He's better at splitting infinitives than he is at looking after his people's affairs. He never renewed the copyright on those stories. We don't owe anyone a penny. And by God,

you show me an author who needs the money. Rolling in it, all of them. Living off their royalties." A final injustice struck him; he smote his forehead. "Anyway, what the devil's it got to do with the widow? She didn't write the stories."

To burn up some of his rage, he struggled down to the cellar with the cartons. His blood drummed wildly. As he unpacked the cartons, dust smoked up to the lightbulbs. The cellar, already dim with its crowd of bookshelves, grew dimmer. He piled the books neatly, sometimes shifting a book from one pile to another, as though playing Patience. When he reached the ace, he stopped. *Tales Beyond Life*, by Damien Damon. It was practically a legend; the book had never been reprinted in its entirety. The find could hardly have been more opportune. The book contained "The Dunning of Diavolo"—exactly what he needed to complete the new Tharne anthology, *Justice From Beyond the Grave*. He knocked lumps of dust from the top of the book, and turned to the tale.

Even in death he would be

recompensed. Might the resurrectionists have his corpse for a toy? Of a certainty— but only once those organs had been removed which his spirit would need, and the Rituals performed. This stipulation he had willed on his death-bed to his son. Unless his corpse was pacified, his curse would rise.

Undeed, had the father's estate been more readily available to clear the son's debts, this might have been an edifying tale of filial piety. Still, on a night when the moon gleamed like a sepulture, the father was plucked tuber-pallid from the earth. Rather than sow superstitious scruples in the resurrectionists, the son had told them naught. Even so, the burrowers felt that they had mined an uncommon seam. Voiceless it might be, but the corpse had its forms of protest. Only by seizing its wrists could the corpse-miners elude the cold touch of its hands. Could they have closed its stiff lids, they might have borne its grin. On the contrary, neither would touch the gelatinous pebbles which bulged from its face . . .

Tharne knew how the tale continued: Diavolo, the father, was dissected, but his limbs went snaking round the town in search of those who had betrayed him, and crawled down the throats of the victims to drag out the twins of those organs of which the corpse had been robbed. All good Gothic stuff—gory and satisfying, but not to be taken too seriously. They couldn't write like that nowadays; they'd lost the knack of proper Gothic writing. And yet they whined that they weren't paid enough!

Only one thing about the tale annoyed him: the misprint "undeed" for "indeed". Amusingly, it resembled "undead"—but that was no excuse for perpetrating it. The one reprint of the tale, in the twenties, had swarmed with literals. Well, this time the text would be perfect. Nothing appeared in a Tharne anthology until it satisfied him.

He checked the remaining text, then gave it to his secretary to retype. His timing was exact: a minute later the doorbell announced the book collector, who was as punctual as Tharne. They spent a mutually beneficial half-hour. "These I bought only this morning," Tharne said proudly. "They're yours for twenty pounds apiece."

The day seemed satisfactory until the phone rang. He heard the girl's startled squeak. She rang through to his office, sounding flustered. "Ronald Main wants to speak to you."

"Oh God. Tell him to write, if he still knows how. I've no time to waste in chatting, even if he has." But her cry had disturbed him; it sounded like a threat of inefficiency. Let Main see that someone round here wasn't to be shaken! "No, wait—put him on."

Main's orotund voice came rolling down the wire. "It has come to my notice that you have anthologised a story of mine without informing me."

Trust a writer to use as many words as he could! "There was no need to get in touch with you," Tharne said. "The story's out of copyright."

"That is hardly the issue. Aside from the matter of payment, which we shall certainly discuss, I want to take up with you the question of the text itself. Are you aware that whole sentences have been rewritten?"

"Yes, of course. That's part of my job. I am the editor, you know." Irritably Tharne restrained a sneeze; the smell of dust was very strong. "After all, it's an early story of yours. Objectively, don't you think I've improved it?" He oughtn't to sound as if he was weakening. "Anyway, I'm afraid that legally you've no rights."

Did that render Main speechless, or was he preparing a stronger attack? It scarcely mattered, for Tharne put down the phone and strode down the hall to check his secretary's work. Was her typing as flustered as her voice had been?

Her office was hazy with floating dust. No wonder she was peering closely at the book—though she looked engrossed, almost entranced. As his shadow fell on the page she started; the typewriter carriage sprang to its limit, ringing. She demanded "Was that you before?"

"What do you mean?"

"Oh, nothing. Don't let it bother you." She seemed

nervously annoyed— whether with him or with herself he couldn't tell. At least her typing was accurate, though he could see where letters had had to be retyped.

He might as well write the introduction to the story. He went down to fetch *Who's Who in Horror and Fantasy Fiction*. Dust teemed around the cellar lights and chafed his throat. Here was Damien Damon, real name Sidney Drew: b. Chelsea, 30 April 1876; d.? 1911? "His life was even more bizarre and outrageous than his fiction. Some critics say that that is the only reason for his fame . . ." A small dry sound made Tharne glance up. Somewhere among the shelved books, a face peered at him through a gap. Of course it could be nothing of the sort, but it took him a while to locate a cover that had fallen open in a gap and must have resembled a face.

Upstairs he wrote the introduction. ". . . Without the help of an agent, and with no desire to make money from his writing, Damon became one of the most discussed in whispers writers of his day. Critics claim that it was

scandals that he practised magic which gained him fame. But his posthumously published *Tales Beyond Life* shows that he was probably the last really first-class writer in the tradition of Poe . . ." Glancing up, Tharne caught sight of himself, pen in hand, at the desk in the mirror. So much for any nonsense that he didn't understand writers' problems! Why, he was a writer himself!

Only when he'd finished writing did he notice how quiet the house had become. It had the strained unnatural silence of a library. As he padded down the hall to deliver the text to his secretary his sounds felt muffled, detached from him. His secretary was poring over the typescript of Damon's tale. She looked less efficient than anxious— searching for something she would rather not find? Dust hung about her in the amber light, and made her resemble a waxwork or a faded painting. Her arms dangled, forgotten. Her gaze was fixed on the page.

Before he could speak, the phone rang. That startled her so badly that he thought his presence might dismay her more. He retreated into the hall, and a dark shape stepped back behind him—his shadow, of course. He entered her office once more, making sure he was audible. "It's Mr Main again," she said, almost wailing.

"Tell him to put it in writing."

"Mr. Tharne says would you please send him a letter." Her training allowed her to regain control, yet she seemed unable to put down the phone until instructed. Tharne enjoyed the abrupt cessation of the outraged squeaking. "Now I think you'd better go home and get some rest," he said.

Once she'd left he sat at her desk and read the typescripts. Yes, she had corrected the original; "undeed" was righted. The text seemed perfect, ready for the printer. Why then did he feel that something was wrong? Had she omitted a passage or otherwise changed the wording? He'd compare the texts in his office, where he was more comfortable. As he rose, he noticed a few faint dusty marks on the carpet. They approached behind his secretary's chair, then veered away. He must have tracked dust from the cellar, which clearly needed sweeping. What did his housekeeper think she was paid for?

Again his footsteps sounded muted. Perhaps his ears were clogged with dust; there was certainly enough of it about. He had never noticed how strongly the house smelled of old books, nor how unpleasant the smell could be. His skin felt dry, itchy. In his office he poured himself a large Scotch. It was late enough, he needn't feel guilty—indeed, twilight seemed unusually swift tonight, unless it was an effect of the swarms of dust. He didn't spend all day drinking, unlike some writers he could name.

He knocked clumps of dust from the book; it seemed almost to grow there, like grey fungus. Airborne dust whirled away from him and drifted back. He compared the texts, line by line. Surely they were identical, except for her single correction. Yet he felt there was some aspect of the typescript which he needed urgently to decipher. This frustration, and its irrationality, unnerved him.

He was still frowning at the pages, having refilled his glass to loosen up his thoughts, when the phone rang once. He grabbed it irritably, but the earpiece was as hushed as the house. Or was there, amid the electric hissing vague as a cascade of dust, a whisper? It was beyond the grasp of his hearing, except for a syllable or two which sounded like Latin—if it was there at all.

He jerked to his feet and hurried down the hall. Now that he thought about it, perhaps he'd heard his secretary's extension lifted as his phone had rung. Yes, her receiver was off the hook. It must have fallen off. As he replaced it, dust sifted out of the mouthpiece. Was a piece of paper rustling in the hall? No, the hall was bare. Perhaps it was the typescript, stirred on his desk by a draught. He closed the door behind him, to exclude any draught—as well as the odour of something very old and dusty.

The smell was stronger in his room. He sniffed gingerly at *Tales Beyond Life*. Why, there it was: the book reeked of dust. He shoved open the French windows, then he sat and stared at the typescript. He was beginning to regard it with positive dislike. He felt as though he had been given a code to crack; it was nerve-racking as an examination. Why was it only the typescript that bothered him, and not the original?

He flapped the typed pages, for they looked thinly coated with grey. Perhaps it was only the twilight, which seemed composed of dust. Even his Scotch tasted clogged. Just let him see what was wrong with this damned story, then he'd leave the room to its dust— and have a few well-chosen words for his housekeeper tomorrow.

There was only one difference between the texts: the capital I. Or had he missed another letter? Compulsively and irritably, refusing to glance at the grey lump which hovered at the edge of his vision, he checked the first few capitals. E, M, O, R, T . . . Suddenly he stopped, parched mouth open. Seizing his pen, he began to transcribe the capitals alone.

E mortuis revoco.

From the dead I summon thee.

Oh, it must be a joke, a mistake, a coincidence. But the next few capitals dashed his doubts. *From the dead I summon thee, from the dust I recreate thee* . . . The entire story concealed a Latin invocation. It had been Damien Damon's last story and also, apparently, his last attempt at magic.

And it was Tharne's discovery. He must rewrite his introduction. Publicised correctly, the secret of the tale could help the book's sales a great deal. Why then was he unwilling to look up? Why was he tense as a trapped animal, ears straining painfully? Because of the thick smell of dust, the stealthy dry noises that his choked ears were unable to locate, the grey mass that hovered in front of him?

When at last he managed to look up, the jerk of his head twinged his neck. But his gasp was of relief. The grey blotch was only a chunk of dust, clinging to the mirror. Admittedly it was unpleasant; it resembled a face masked with dust, which also spilled from the face's dismayingly numerous openings. Really, he could live without it, much as he resented having to do his housekeeper's job for her. When he rose, it took

him a moment to realise that his reflection had partly blotted out the grey mass. In the further moment before he understood, two more reflected grey lumps rose beside it, behind him. Were they hands or wads of dust? Perhaps they were composed of both. It was impossible to tell, even when they closed over his face.

©
Story: Ramsey Campbell
Art: Rick McCollum

Ramsey Campbell was born in Liverpool in 1946 and now lives in Wallasey. The *Oxford Companion to English Literature* describes him as "Britain's most respected living horror writer", and the *Washington Post* sums up his work as "one of the monumental accomplishments of modern popular fiction". He has received the Grand Master Award of the World Horror Convention, the Lifetime Achievement Award of the Horror Writers Association, the Living Legend Award of the International Horror Guild and the World Fantasy Lifetime Achievement Award. In 2015 he was made an Honorary Fellow of Liverpool John Moores University for outstanding services to literature. PS Publishing have brought out two volumes of *Phantasmagorical Stories*, a sixty-year retrospective of his short fiction, and a companion collection, *The Village Killings and Other Novellas*, while their Electric Dreamhouse imprint has his collected film reviews, *Ramsey's Rambles*. His latest novel is *Fellstones* from Flame Tree Press, who have also recently published his Brichester Mythos trilogy.

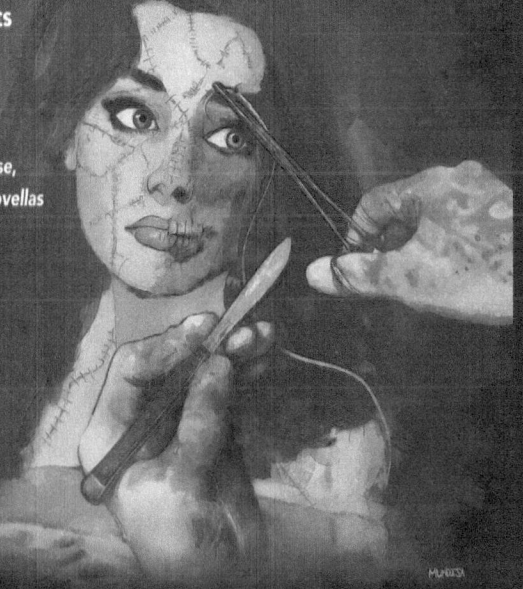

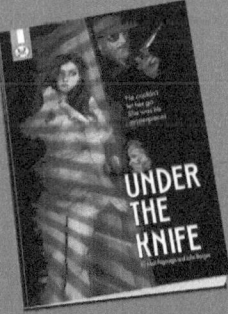

She'd asked him once if it were possible to run out of energy altogether.
"The nearest sun would have to disappear," he'd said.

Devil's Alley

Wendy Velasquez

Korina Martinez-Tinajero ignored him at first. Loch had said, "There's something moving starboard, coming in quick." He'd tried, since they'd left Earth, to put the moves on her. She dismissed his comment as another attempt to scare her into thinking their lives might be threatened ("Let's get in one last good one," he'd said the previous times he'd pointed to gas formations outside the ship while they tore through nebulae. The first one he called a cosmic ghost, capable of gumming the works in the electromagnetic engine and leaving them stranded in space. The last two, he claimed, were demon gods surfing star systems in search of anything resembling meat). She explained, over and over, as patiently as possible, their relationship began and ended with business. Nothing more. Her father, who'd paid for the expedition, insisted she contract the grimy, near-convicted dope smuggler to fly the ship. She begged her father to purchase a simulated human programmed for inter-stellar navigation. He insisted Loch would teach her valuable lessons about life outside the *privilegiado*. Loch Junak had transported Elgin's Spirit, a hallucinogenic drug from the Prosser system to Earth and sold it to his own people, the *trabajadores*. When she asked her father why in the world they should trust a criminal, her father repeated his wish that she learn about the struggles of those who had not been born with gold-coated diapers.

Loch jabbed his filthy, grease-coated finger at the window to his right. "Have yourself a peek."

Soaring beasts of oil-black, fleshy material shifted and wound through the blackness in Devil's Alley. The galaxy had actually been named

Welker-22, after Shannon Welker, the astronomer who discovered it in the 21st century. The planets within were given similar, boring designations—Welker-67, Welker-68, and so on. Korina and her pilot were headed for Welker-71, a planet twice the size of Earth and begging for a prospector to claim the rights to sell to the highest bidding corporation back home. Her father had agreed to split the net profit from the expedition. She would be able to retire before thirty.

Loch had re-christened the Welker system Devil's Alley after pointing out how the five planets within revolved around the sun in the pattern of a pentagram. Old world, *trabajadores* humor—acting like the dead religions of the ancient Middle East still had relevance.

"Could be debris," she said.

"They're moving with us, Korina," he said. "Looks deliberate."

Ugh. Did she have to tell him again? "Ma'am," she said. "I've asked you a hundred times now, call me ma'am. I sign your paycheck." *¡Qué fastidio!*, her servants on Earth understood how to take orders. Loch would have spent his life in a correction facility on Io if her father hadn't vouched for him, promised him work. That was a heck of lot more than most *trabajadores* were granted and most of them, technically, weren't criminals.

"Yeah, well, in case you didn't notice, *ma'am*," said Loch, "they've gotten a whole lot closer these last few minutes." He looked at her without facing her, tilting his head in an arrogant sneer. The *nerve.*

She stared at him, held out her arms. "And?" She hated when people didn't say exactly what they meant to say. *Trabajadores* often played this game. She assumed it gave their lives meaning, turning minute conversation into mystery.

"Those things out there," he said, "whatever they are, they're headed toward '71, exactly where we're going."

"Keep tabs on them." She closed her eyes, shut off her natural, neural functions, and summoned a magazine from her identity chip. She flipped through the latest issue of

Lujoso, marveling at mansions on the shores of China and India, where old money still lived like royalty. She examined the latest fashions digital movie stars in Hong Kong were flaunting. Looked a bit like a throwback to the 2150s. The skirts were quite conservative, still covering at least three inches of the women's thighs. They wore tops over their bras as well. Amusing.

Their ship, christened *El Viaje* by her father, had gained speed since they'd entered Devil's Alley. Loch had explained to her, months ago, how the electromagnetic engine worked. The closer they were to a star, the more energy the engine absorbed. Between solar systems, the ship operated on reserve. She'd asked him once if it were possible to run out of energy altogether. "The nearest sun would have to disappear," he'd said.

The panels above her and to her side rattled. She swiped the magazine from her mind and returned her attention to material reality. "You're going to break this thing into pieces." Was he trying to scare her again? *¡Qué fastidio!*, why couldn't her father have hired a simulated human to pilot the ship?

Loch leaned back and nodded toward the portal over his shoulder. "They're not friendly, whatever they are."

Flocks of creatures she could only compare to headless bats the size of antique, compact automobiles flapped their thick, leathery wings at impossible angles. The insides of their wings were covered with gaping holes filled with teeth as sharp as butcher knives, as though they had dozens of mouths chomping, for whatever reason, at *El Viaje*. "What are they?" she said.

"Never seen anything like them." Loch smiled. "They sure look hungry, don't they?" He pushed the throttle controlling the amount of power the engine produced. The ship rocked back and shot forward toward the planet in front of them. The floor shook and the bolts holding Korina's seat in place wobbled.

She grabbed the armrests on both sides of her and squeezed. If this turned out to be some sort of trick, she'd have Loch Junak neutered the moment they stepped foot on Earth. When her father showed her *El Viaje* for the first time, she'd complained it looked like an old tin can getting ready to fall apart. Despite his having acquired it from a scrap dealer in Amarillo, he assured her the technology was sound. The World Government had rejected electromagnetic engines in 2160, claiming only rogue corporations and criminals had any use for them. "The truth is," her father had said, "sometimes our leaders don't know what's best for us." He explained how nuclear-powered space travel, preferred by the masses, was slow and energy-consuming. "The EM models are much faster, much more efficient. The major corporations can't make money off of something that works too well, so they've paid for them to be discredited." That didn't change her impression, however, as she'd run her hands over the clumsy exterior. The ship resembled a bottle, the kind from which the *trabajadores* drank their unhealthy, alcoholic sodas. The engine flowered at the

tail end, its copper blades resembling the propeller on an ancient submarine. The whole thing reminded her of drawings she'd seen of early interpretations of rockets, before rockets had actually been invented.

El Viaje jerked hard to the left. Korina looked out her window. The planet was directly beneath her, the reflection of the sun now bright enough to blind her. "Loch!" she said. A metallic bang rocked the middle of the ship, where the artificial gravity wheel spun like the motor on an antique clock her father kept in his study. The gray wings of the creatures outside flapped silently around the ship, knocking it side to side, as though playing ping-pong with it. She tried, one last time, to convince herself the mangy pirate operating the ship had somehow conspired with these aliens to scare her, literally, out of her pants.

"Hold on," he said.

The bottom of the ship rumbled as the captain barrel rolled it until finding orbit. The creatures hopped and skipped off the edge of the planet's atmosphere. Then the back of the ship rattled. The clanging of the beast's wings smashing into the engine filled the cabin with high-pitched bangs, like a dozen men pounding a sheet of aluminum into unnatural shapes.

Korina turned to look out the small portals near the rear. They were covered with the hideous sight of the open mouths on the creature's wings swiping at the ship with their sword-like fangs. She knew women who would have crumbled right then, staring directly into the void of mortality, but she walked taller than her peers. Her father had taken her hunting on Mars when she was twelve. They shot political dissidents for sport on the Red Planet. These were no easy marks. The criminals they stalked were armed as well and desperate to survive.

Loch worked the computer on his side of the control panel. "Just got to find a nice place to slip inside." He winked at her. "Get nice and cozy, see if these sons of bitches can take the heat."

The ship continued to pick up speed as it surfed the arc of the planet. Between *El Viaje*'s jittery construction and the molestations taking place on the exterior, Korina couldn't help but imagine the ship breaking into pieces. Would she black out before the pressure of space popped her like a balloon? She'd ignored thoughts of death to that point. Now, it seemed as close as the ends of her fingers.

"Here we go." Loch typed numbers into the computer. He grabbed the wheel between his legs and eased the ship toward a minor break in the stream of gases flowing around them.

El Viaje sank into the atmosphere like a train going over the first hill on a roller coaster. Korina's stomach rose into her throat. They'd gone through this on the three planets they'd already explored and claimed. It never failed to thrill her as fire engulfed the outside of the ship and they dropped, screaming toward the surface.

Despite Loch's grip on it, the wheel convulsed into a blur. Everything, in fact, had doubled before Korina's eyes. She heard the captain release his guttural, smutty laugh. He said, "Take that, you sons of bitches!"

Korina glanced out her window. The creatures were repelled, one by one, by flames and sparks skating off the exterior of the ship. As the atmosphere blended into the lime sky over Welker-71, the foul beasts, whatever they were, disappeared into space.

It usually took twenty minutes for Loch to bring the ship's momentum to a tolerable speed after entry. They flew through vanilla clouds, over spiked, snow-capped mountain ranges with lush, violet and turquois growth at their bases. The glorious work of nature, untouched by humanity's greedy, industrious fingers. As they swung out over a sea, the water just as clear as a priceless emerald from the museums in Mexico City, Korina wondered, as she always did when seeing another virgin planet, whether her trade suffered an ethical deficit. In the service of saving humanity from the broken Earth, would her species repeat their mistakes, leaving charred stones across the galaxy?

The ship slowed, banked, and descended toward a body of land with what appeared to be a terrain of crimson, sand-like soil. "Not bad," said Loch. He stared out the portals overhead. He looked so smug Korina wanted to kick him. Such a throwback, a man who believed he could flaunt his limited intelligence in the face of a superior, a *woman*, no less. He would become rich as well, as a result of the expedition, but if Korina had her way, he'd be hanged for his arrogance.

Something nagged her, dis-tracted her from her delicious hatred of the captain—"Will they bother us when we leave?"

The captain tilted his head. "I wish I knew, Korina . . ." He held up one hand, as if to stop her before she scolded him. "Ma'am, I apologize. I wish I knew, *ma'am*."

Loch insisted they wear flight suits and oxygen masks when they exited the ship. The ground gave a bit when they walked on it, felt like stepping on a sea of boiled cornmeal. Few signs of life grew in the desert. Trees with pitch black trunks and burnt green leaves drooping off their branches bent under the weight of the atmosphere. They looked like people crouched over to pull plants from the soil. Aside from occasional rodent-like mammals with six legs scampering from one hole in the ground to the next, there appeared to be no animals capable of competing for vital resources.

They trudged for several miles. Korina took photographs to include in her sales package when she returned to Earth and began taking bids from corporations. She documented royal blue lakes and gray cloud patterns painting the land in dark, monochrome shades. Frankly, the planet didn't look as impressive up close as it had from the sky. That wouldn't matter to the people back home. The *trabajadores*, the poor masses who were lucky to find work fixing machines for the *privilegiado*, were desperate to leave Earth.

As they returned to the ship, the shadows created by the clouds shifted as though hands above them were shuffling pieces of a jigsaw puzzle. Loch fiddled with the compressor

on his oxygen tank. "Damn thing," he said. "I can tell there's a leak somewhere."

Korina shielded her eyes from the faint sun. High above the lime-colored sky, black objects swarmed closer and closer together. She pointed it out to Loch. "You think they'll give up, eventually?"

He stared at them for some time. "Stubborn sons of bitches, aren't they?" He examined the tubes leading to his oxygen mask. "Here it is." He tapped his finger on the left tube. He said they had to reach the ship by nightfall. "No telling how cold it's going to get."

They followed the sunken imprints their feet had made on the land back to *El Viaje*. The number of beasts squirming above the planet's atmosphere had increased, as though they had called every living member of their species to hound them. Inside the ship, Loch insisted Korina give him her oxygen mask. "I need to patch the engine before night hits." He promised they'd take off in the morning, provided she stayed out of his way.

She sat in her seat in the cockpit, closed her eyes, and

loaded a television show she'd stored in her identity chip. *Penelope Pesado*, a telenovela, told the story of a *privilegiado* woman trying to hold on to her wealth and find romance amidst protests and attempted coups by the local *trabajadores*. She'd seen every episode multiple times since leaving the Earth. She eventually became bored and opened her mind back to reality. A massive shadow had fallen over *El Viaje* for a half mile in every direction. She strained to peer out the skylight portal. A black mass had formed overhead, beyond the clouds. She found the captain's malfunctioning oxygen mask in the equipment hatch and put it on. As soon as she stepped out, she realized the damage to the mask had been worse than Loch had indicated. Her lungs heaved, attempting to pull in what fragments of air the broken tube allowed. Worse, however, a series of high-pitched shrills rained down from above. The beasts had made no sound in space, but their spine-grating cries found purchase in the planet's atmosphere. They resembled hawks, on Earth,

screeching before snatching prey from a brown field of dead grass or a polluted lake. She hurried to the rear of the ship.

Loch used a small laser to weld the seams of the steel plates protecting the engine. Deep gashes, where the beasts had sunk their teeth, decorated the exterior. She tapped his shoulder and directed his attention, once more, to the gathering creatures in space.

"I know," he said. "My guess is they're guarding the sun, preventing us from stealing its energy." He tried to continue fixing the ship.

"But," she said, "we're going to be able to get past them?"

He turned off the laser and rested for a moment. "Korina… *Ma'am*, my apologies. Depending on how many of those things there are, we may not be leaving here. Ever."

Bastardo. Even now, he couldn't control himself. "You try this nonsense one more time," she said, "I'll see to it you're sent to Io as soon as we get back to Earth, really. So help me, you even think about putting your hands on me, I'll cut them off."

The man didn't shiver,

shake, or react in any way other than a slight grin. He flipped the switch on the laser and resumed gluing the ship together. Korina marched back to the cabin, afraid her anger might complicate her breathing. No man among the *privilegiado* would ever be so smug to a woman. For whatever reason, wealth taught the weaker sex their proper place. She plopped down in her seat in the cockpit, arms folded in front of her, and watched the black ring surrounding them widen until their side of the planet turned away from the sun. She should have been tired, should have retreated to her sleeping quarters. Her heart, which had been racing since the captain had made his latest attempt to bed her, refused to slow. The land turned dark. Three moons orbiting the planet reflected the sun and pierced the terrain with a burgundy glow. Eventually, that glorious illumination was stolen by the gathering beasts. Korina began to miss the captain, for no other reason than she wanted someone to listen to her concerns.

Just as she felt she could no longer keep her eyes open, as though her rising fear had exhausted her, Loch opened the hatch and climbed into the ship. Frost covered his mask and flight suit. He unzipped the clunky, orange one-piece and stepped out of it, shivering. "Colder than you know what," he said.

"No, I don't."

"Well, it's cold. Let me tell you." He stepped toward the back of the ship and held his hands near the panels leading to the engine, rubbing them the way one might warm themselves by a campfire.

Outside, the world had turned pitch black.

"Afraid we're going to have to conserve the ship's energy, rely on our own body heat." Loch twisted dials on the engine panels all the way to the left. "Those things have blocked out the sun completely."

Korina stared at him. Was he still trying to get fresh with her? Even *now*? She surmised, for the first time, how ragged he went through life. His pants were baggy, far too big for him. His shirt had holes in the elbows. He didn't seem to mind these things, didn't seem to care the *privilegiados* would judge him for his poverty. Once rich, would he change this about himself? Would he take pride in his appearance? Would he understand how to *be* wealthy?

"Why don't you get yourself some shut-eye," he said. He patted the fiberglass door to her sleeping quarters. "I'll keep watch."

She grabbed her shoulders. "I don't feel like sleeping."

"Tomorrow could be a big day." He winked at her.

¡Qué fastidio! She thought about slapping him. "I'm fine right here." She focused on the window in front of her, which had become opaque. The cries from the beasts above echoed across the darkness, interrupted what would otherwise be perfect calm and silence. Whichever corporation bought the rights to Welker-71 would have to exterminate the creatures before settling the planet.

The captain pulled a dinner tray from the food supply and sat in his chair munching on a cube of artificial steak and vegetables. Every so often, he'd turn to her and ask if she were hungry, if she needed anything. His voice had changed. In previous moments of possible distress, he'd spoken in snarky, smug tones, as though he expected his scare tactics to work. Now, he sounded more like a parent, concerned about a child's wellbeing. Condescending, yes. Didactic, yes. The change worried her, though. He carried the air of a man unsure of his next move.

Korina eventually slipped into an uncomfortable sleep, constantly shifting to compensate for her awkward position. She'd lean to her right, open her eyes, see the captain picking his nose or chewing one of his fingernails, and move to the other side. Eventually, she'd wake, slightly, see the darkened windows, shake as though someone had walked on her grave, and roll back. After several hours of this, she gave up. The captain, however, had fallen into what appeared to be a pleasant slumber. He'd rested his head in his hand and snored like a chainsaw turned on and off, over and over again. An obscene noise she'd been spared for most of the trip. She watched him for a while, began to think of him as a human being. Then she realized the ship had gotten unbearably cold.

"Hey," she said. She knocked his hand from his chin.

Loch nearly fell out of his seat. He blinked, an indignant look on his face. "What . . . ?" He gawked at her the way she might throw darts with her eyes at a servant who had overcooked her breakfast.

"It's freezing." She expected him to understand he needed to get off his butt and turn up the heat.

The captain looked at the control panel in front of him. "It's been dark for sixteen hours now," he said. He got out of his chair and stumbled to the engine panels. He glanced back at Korina. He showed her an expression she'd never seen from him. If she didn't know better, she would have sworn his wide eyes and deep breathing signified fear.

"What's going on?" she said.

He put on his flight suit and strapped an oxygen mask to his face.

She smacked her hands together with each word she spoke: "I asked you a question."

"Ma'am," he said, "the engine is dead." He opened the side door and stepped out.

Korina pulled her flight suit from the equipment hatch and put on the broken oxygen mask. She followed the captain outside the ship. He walked in a circle around *El Viaje*, staring up the entire time. The sky had been completely blotted out by the creatures flying overhead. They'd clustered so tightly, no sunlight could penetrate.

"Looks like you got your wish," she said.

He drew his head back, as though he had no idea what she meant.

"Looks like we're doomed."

"Maybe," he said. "We'll see who's more patient."

The cold infiltrated Korina's flight suit, let her know how uncomfortable she'd be from then until the moment her body could take it no more.

Wendy Velasquez is a poet hiding in the middle of Los Angeles. Her fiction and verse have appeared in several publications, including *Hidden Gems*, *Pulp Modern*, *Rat Potato Pie*, and *Genesis II*.

©
Story: Wendy Velasquez
Art: Rick McCollum

*"Welcome to the Yellow House! You will love it here!
Everything is always wonderful and perfect!"*

The Yellow House

Lisa Voorhees

When Marla's best friend Jette insisted she take a vacation, the first place her friend mentioned was the Yellow House. Set out in the country at the end of a dirt road, summer light shining off the clapboard siding, the house was yellow all right.

Bright yellow, like the dozens of dandelions populating the surrounding yard, which spread out over a perfectly manicured lawn with rolling hills covered in emerald green grass.

The bus dropped Marla off and sped away down the road, leaving a dust cloud the size of a small tornado in its wake. She fidgeted with the strap on her beat-up leather messenger bag and stared up at the place. The windows were like dark scars on the face of what might have been a cheerful house, three lifetimes of paint jobs ago.

"What the hell, Jette? Is this some kind of joke?" Jette's parents owned the house and rented it out on occasion. Apparently, that didn't happen frequently and quite frankly, it wasn't hard to see why. Not that Marla would ever say anything disparaging to her friend's face. Jette wasn't one for putting a negative spin on things, so Marla had learned to force herself to stop, think positively, and smother her cynicism behind a plastic smile of satisfaction.

"A little slice of heaven," she muttered, "out in the middle of nowhere. It'll be great, just the vacation I need."

Marla reached for a cigarette and lit up, sucking in the nicotine haze, one anxious drag at a time. Fraternizing with the bus driver was more social contact than she was used to enduring and all the quaint conversation had drained her. She could only fake smile through the stream of idle chit chat for so long before her mind started to

get the jitters and that fluttery feeling in her chest threatened to rob her of air.

She hated calling them panic attacks. It was people who unnerved her, the need to make conversation when all she wanted was a quiet, safe space to let her mind unpack itself so she could see what was there, maybe reorganize things differently, see if they made more sense in another configuration.

Lately, some distance had grown between her and Jette. They'd been best friends since second grade, but Jette couldn't handle the recent shit going on in her life. The fire. Marla's parents, both dead. *Struggles grow you, or else they kill you.* That's what her dad always said, and he was right.

Problem was, they had grown Marla in ways Jette had yet to experience. Her best friend's bubble of innocence hadn't broken, that day-to-day feeling that things are going all right, nothing much could touch her because all the bad shit was happening to someone else, the poor bastard, and her world was basically stable.

Jette had arranged this vacation because she was worried about her friend being depressed. Stupid sloth that she was, Marla had humored her.

Too late to back out, now that she was here. She climbed the squeaky wooden stairs to the front porch and read the words on the painted plastic doormat.

BE HAPPY.

Stylized bluebirds and shiny red hearts completed the kitsch ensemble. "Whatever," she mumbled, flashing a wry smile. Attached to a spiral cord, the key was indeed under the loathsome mat, as Jette had promised it would be.

Marla stamped out her cigarette and flung it out into the yard. Probably didn't allow smoking in a rental. It seemed more like a deadbeat campus listing for cheap student housing than a destination spot, but that was beside the point.

It was the thought that counted, and Jette was a better friend to her than anyone else so she was willing to play along.

She unlocked the door, slipped the keychain on her

wrist, and cruised around the joint. Once Jette arrived, she'd have to put on her game face and pretend like she was having *a really good time!*

The interior was remarkably pristine, compared to the outside. She'd even go so far as to call it posh, though Marla was no designer. She wouldn't recognize a couture piece of furniture if it hit her in the face.

Red couches sat in the living room, with a glass-topped coffee table enmeshed in a shaggy white throw rug. Mirrors hung everywhere. The dining room was painted a forest green. After the disconcerting effect of the mirrors, the dark color had a calming effect on her.

The bedrooms were as impressive as the rest of the house. The room with the polka dot wallpaper was the one closest to the stairs, so she chose it. Marla had a thing about being able to escape. In restaurants, she always chose the seat with the best view of the door, in case of emergencies. A vacation was no different.

She sank down on the bed and considered texting Jette.

The place wasn't a complete dump, no matter what the outside looked like, though she could hardly phrase it that way. She snapped her fingers in the air, thinking.

It's so awesome. We're going to have such a great time!

No.

You're the best, Jette! I love the place.

Still . . . no.

Can't wait until you get here! Hurry up!

Ugh. No.

Why was it always such a struggle to play the Jette game? It should be easier than it was. Marla rolled her eyes and flopped back on the pillows.

The house key at her wrist jangled and her heart gave a weird little flutter. She sat up and stared at the flat surface of the window. What in hell's name was wrong with the clouds? Perfect little symmetric white puff balls in a pale blue sky, they hadn't shifted since she stepped inside the room.

Dandelions dotted the rolling green hills but in addition to those, a host of red tulips and white daffodils had sprung up in rows like prize-winning entries at a flower show.

Her gaze latched onto a bird in the sky. It was some distance away, but yet, the bird didn't appear to move.

Marla slid off the bed and approached the window. The view out of the other window was much the same. Perfect, idyllic, and still.

Stagnant.

She got up real close to the glass and pressed her cheek against it. Her view of the outside didn't shift, as it should have with her change in perspective. This tableau, this artifact of perfection, wasn't real.

Something had been attached to the outside of the window, some kind of decal or false veneer. Maybe if she checked the other windows in the house, she would find out it was just this one, that it had been a kid's room.

Marla investigated upstairs, then raced downstairs and examined the rest of those rooms' windows, too. All were covered in the exact same veneer. A plastic definition of reality, painted across every transparent surface of the house, blocking her view of the outside world.

Her heart slammed against her ribs as she ran down the hall toward the front door. She had to get outside and get a breath of fresh air.

She rattled the knob, but it wouldn't budge. The door didn't have a lock on this side, only the bare knob and a brass plate where a lock should have been.

"What the fuck?" She hated how shook up she sounded. She forced herself to take a deep breath, then tried the back door and next, all the windows. She couldn't open a single one.

A hysterical laugh escaped her chest. She ran trembling fingers through her hair and paced the hall a few times, then wandered into the kitchen for a drink from the tap.

In the cupboard, she discovered a bottle of champagne and a gift basket. Wedged among the bright green Easter grass was a batch of perfectly ripe, flawless bananas and a chocolate disc wrapped in yellow foil printed with a huge smiley face.

She broke off a piece of the chocolate and nibbled on a corner. It was utterly tasteless, like cardboard, so she spat it out in the sink and tried a banana. Might as well have been styrofoam.

Marla considered forcing down another mouthful of tasteless chocolate when the doorbell rang.

She proceeded down the tiled hall, contemplating the likelihood that Jette had caught an early train out of the city. Except why would Jette ring the bell? She should have a spare key.

The mail slot rattled and Marla hesitated. Someone was forcing a padded brown envelope through. It fell to the floor with a small thud. Afterward, the mail slot slammed shut.

"Wait!" She attempted to prise the mail slot open, tearing her nails in the process. "Hang on, please! The door won't open. I need help."

A response never came.

Defeated, she dropped to the ground and flipped the package over. Her name was printed in black marker on the front, followed by THE YELLOW HOUSE, and no return address.

Marla tore open the envelope and pulled out a box wrapped in plastic. Several dozen packets of gum were layered in neat columns with the words Befuddlement gum written across their labels. She shook the envelope and a yellow note card emblazoned with a rainbow and cherry colored hearts dropped out.

Inside the card, in nondescript handwriting, someone had written, WELCOME TO THE YELLOW HOUSE! YOU WILL LOVE IT HERE! EVERYTHING IS ALWAYS WONDERFUL AND PERFECT!

Perfect, her ass.

Marla couldn't think of anything worse actually. Jette wasn't here and she was locked inside the Yellow House with nothing but tasteless food to sustain her until she could find a way out. She slid a hand over her eyes, pressing her fingers against the lids. This was supposed to be a vacation. Shouldn't Jette be here with her to experience it?

Sprawled out on the bed in the polka dot room, Marla contemplated lighting up. Jette wasn't answering her phone, and Marla's jitters had picked up. The lights were off, but sleep wasn't happening.

Marla sighed and dragged

her arm across her eyes. The window veneers were getting to her. The red tulips on the hillside were crisp red, the white clouds eternally still. Lifeless.

That's when she noticed them, the polka dots on the wallpaper starting to wiggle. Like particles in Brownian motion, they shivered and jerked side to side, some of them with little smiles on their faces. Their delicate laughter filled the room, growing louder.

She sat up and stared at them, expecting the illusion to fade the longer she concentrated on them, willing them not to be a thing. The longer she stared at them, the harder they laughed, like kids bent over silly, lost in the throes of hysterics.

Her gaze darted to the open doorway, and the hall beyond. She'd picked this room on purpose; the stairs were inches away.

Under her feet, the wooden steps creaked. The house groaned, its walls wavering inward as if underwater, dappled light playing across the surfaces.

Marla tripped and tumbled against the front door frame.

She couldn't help but chuckle. If she was the final girl in a slasher, the Yellow House didn't stand a chance. Except this wasn't a horror flick and she was no blood-spattered actress. She smashed her fists on the door, screamed until her throat was raw, then repeated the same effort with each of the windows.

It was useless. She worked her fingers in circles over her temples. A cigarette. She just needed a smoke.

Back upstairs, Marla shuffled down the hall and settled on the edge of the bed. Her cigarettes lay on the nightstand next to the box that had been delivered earlier. When she reached for the carton, her hand closed around a pack of Befuddlement gum instead.

Her freaking cigarettes. While she'd been running all over the Yellow House desperate to flee, the polka dot freak show had stolen the last of her gaspers.

It didn't matter. She didn't need a fix that bad. She would get through this, polka dots be damned. They could sing and laugh all they wanted.

With shaking fingers, she unwrapped a piece of gum

and popped it in her mouth. A minty splash coated her tongue and wound its way through her nostrils. She sagged back against the pillows, breathing in the scent.

A moment later, the dance of the polka dots wasn't nearly so irksome; it was entertaining. She laughed, spun a finger in the air. The house key dangled from her wrist. She tore it off, wondering what had possessed her to keep such a tight hold on it. The view from the upstairs windows was amazing.

The flowers swayed so gracefully. The longer she watched, the more their gentle movements lulled her into a stupor. It didn't occur to her to wonder how a veneer could move. She was too wrapped up in the taste of sweet milk chocolate, the same tasteless candy she had eaten earlier, lingering on her tongue.

Marla may have slept. The Befuddlement gum made it hard to tell. The comforter was feather light beneath her, like nestling inside a cloud. The patterns in the textured ceiling swirled above, invisible brushstrokes on a swarming, all-white canvas. She sat up and caught a reflection of herself in the stand mirror set in the corner.

What a goofy smile plastered across her face!

She stuck out her tongue and fell back against the covers, laughing. This house was hilarious and fun. She should have realized it sooner. Never mind the gnawing emptiness deep inside, a fresh stick of gum would dull that sensation, too.

Downstairs, the rotary phone in the kitchen started ringing. The old-timey jangle simultaneously roused her curiosity and sent a frisson of apprehension up her spine. She popped a fresh piece of gum in her mouth, relishing the minty infusion, the disconnection from any unpleasantness that threatened to kill her newfound euphoria.

She would go see who it was!

But she would keep the gum with her, the packet pressed reassuringly against her palm. She jogged downstairs and approached the phone, which jumped against the cradle each time it rang.

"Hello?"

"Jette? Is that you?"

"Of course it's me."

It sounded like a badly recorded version of Jette rather than the real thing. Her voice had a faint mechanical buzz to it, like static.

"How do you like the Yellow House so far?"

Marla fumbled with the wrapper on another stick of gum and savored the minty bliss for a few chews. "It's so fantastic!"

She opened the refrigerator door, surprised to discover a box of frozen waffles inside, along with a bottle of syrup and a bowl of fresh strawberries.

It occurred to her that something was missing, there was something she was forgetting to tell Jette. The gum did nothing for her memory, but then again, it trumped feeling like every new situation was an emergency she had to run from.

Jette couldn't see her hasty fake smile. "This was a great vacation idea."

Her gaze lifted to the window.

To that damned veneer with the same rolling hills, the too colorful flowers, and the dripping yellow sunshine.

None of it had changed. Every single window was plastered with the same unalterable view, in every room of the house.

That was what she had forgotten to mention.

The gum in her mouth went tasteless, no more than a rubbery wad of nothingness. She spat it out in the sink.

"Jette!"

The phone went dead in her hands. "Are you there? Jette? Come on, answer me." After several long moments of eerie silence, she gave up and slammed the phone back onto the cradle.

"Shit."

At least she knew something about the house's modus operandi. *Chew the Befuddlement gum and everything will be okay.*

Well. Enough of that. She wouldn't eat any more of the gum and she'd keep her sanity, thank you very much.

Marla tossed the packet of gum in her hand into the trash. The bright splash of color warred against the white plastic bag. She shuddered, then threaded her way upstairs to the polka dot room and brought down the entire box of Befuddlement gum.

Into the trash it went. *Thwack.*

Marla fished around for her lighter, lit a flame over the trash, and let go.

The plastic crackled and popped, a fire taking hold.

The phone rang and Marla froze. Jette had hung up the moment Marla had thought about addressing the veneers.

Even if the house had sensed her suspicion and channeled it into Jette, her friend wouldn't bother calling back. She'd be angry as hell, and when Jette was pissed, she shut people out.

The red plastic phone danced on the cradle.

Marla reached for the handle, trembling. She snatched it up before the next jangle erupted. "Hello?"

Ear-splitting static, so loud she had to hold the phone a foot away. From the depths of the nonsense, chilling, robotic laughter surfaced.

"Who is this?" Marla fought to keep her voice steady.

"You know who," the mechanized voice wheezed through the static.

Heat prickled up her spine.

"Is this some kind of joke?"

Again, that laugh. *"You're* the joke, Marla."

"What?"

"You heard me. You came to the Yellow House to escape your worst fears, but they're not going anywhere."

"I don't have to listen to this."

"Oh yes, you do. Your parents are *dead*, Marla. They're never coming back. Did you think you could escape that?"

"No, I . . . that's not why I came. I wanted to hang out with Jette, to have some fun, you know? Shit, I . . ." Marla twisted sweaty fingers against her palms. Her impulse toward honesty both horrified and compelled her. ". . . I just need a friend . . ."

The static hissed. "Do you honestly think anyone will love you the way you are? A depressed, cynical wreck?"

Marla choked. ". . . I . . . no, I'm . . . that's not—"

"You are a *nobody.*"

With a sob, Marla dropped the receiver. Next to her, smoke billowed from the trash. She wet a dish towel and beat out the flames, scrabbling to remove the box of gum from the bottom and tearing the plastic open with her nails.

She ripped open a packet and shoved the gum in her mouth, one piece, then two, as many as she could to give her that blissful fix.

The minty taste washed over her tongue. Soon the euphoria hit and her senses were adrift in the colors of the house, the pleasant swaying of the walls. Marla stuffed her pockets, giggling, packets clenched between her fingers, determined to salvage all the gum she could.

The doorbell rang.

Marla snapped her head up, surprised. "Oh," she said, humming a sappy tune to herself, sock skating down the hall past the living room mirrors, and laughing at her reflection.

At the end of the hallway, she hesitated. The front door swung open. Under the shadows of the porch awning, Jette stared at her.

Her friend's bobbed black hair feathered along her jawline, which she held stiff, her eyes narrowed. A green sundress hung from her shoulders in starched folds. The outside air was dead, a trace of static buzzing among the trees.

"Jette," Marla said, elated. "I'm so glad you're here." She reached for her friend's hands.

Jette brushed her off and stepped inside, then slammed the door shut.

Marla glanced at the door, then shrugged. "Come into the kitchen. Let's eat."

"I couldn't eat if I tried," Jette said, her painted red lips drooped in a pout. "You won't believe what that bastard Sebastian did to me."

Marla tossed her chewed up wad of Befuddlement gum in the trash. When Jette wasn't looking, she unwrapped three new pieces and popped them in her mouth, then sat down across from her friend at the kitchen table.

Jette's face swam before her vision, smiling amidst the dampness that glistened on her cheeks. Why was Jette crying again?

Something about Sebastian.

". . . lying bastard cheated on me after the pool party . . ."

Marla cocked her head, breathed the minty scent in through her nostrils, and kept chewing, harder.

Jette was beautiful when she

was upset.

But why was she upset?

She was gorgeous. Jette could have any guy she wanted. And practically did, though Sebastian was arguably the one she truly loved.

Under the table, Marla unwrapped another piece of gum, folded it between her fingers, and when Marla turned aside, added it to her current wad.

"I mean, it's unforgivable, right? Especially with a bitch like her?" Jette fumed.

Delirious, Marla smiled. If she wasn't careful, the gum would squeeze through her teeth. "I think you should look on the bright side," she crooned. "You're lucky you found out when you did. Imagine if you'd married the guy. It would be so much worse. Just stay positive."

Jette scoffed, her lip curled back in a sneer. "What the hell, Marla?"

Marla held up her hands. "What can I say?" she laughed. "Everything will work out."

"I'm hurting here," Jette pressed her fingers over her heart, her lower lip trembling. "He *hurt* me."

"Just don't worry, is all I'm saying."

"Fuck you, Marla."

Marla unwrapped a fresh stick of Befuddlement gum and partook. "You'll find the silver lining. I know you."

Jette made a sound halfway between a gasp and a gulp. "That's it," she sniffed. Her chair scraped against the floor, and she advanced on Marla, the cold claws of her fingers digging into the tender flesh in the hollow of Marla's arm.

"I don't have time for this," Jette seethed, dragging Marla toward the front door. Packets of gum spilled out of Marla's pockets, littering the floor and skittering across the tile.

At the entrance, Jette stopped, her perfectly manicured eyebrows drawn together, framing her scowl. "When you're ready to be my friend, come back. Until then, I never want to see you again."

Marla stumbled onto the front porch. The door slammed shut behind her.

"Jette. Wait."

Marla banged on the door. "Come on. Of course I'm your friend."

The gum was losing its flavor. She spat it out and scrounged a few new pieces out of their wrappers, biting down on all of them at once.

The second floor window squeaked open. Her messenger bag hit the shrubbery.

Marla stared at her bag, tangled amongst the branches.

The minty swirl lit up her tongue. The paint on the Yellow House really *did* mirror the sunshiney glow of all the dandelions.

A cheery tune struck up in her mind and Marla shouldered her bag, whistling along, headed in the direction of the main road.

"Ah, Jette." She laughed out loud. "You always were too negative for your own good."

Lisa Voorhees has recently been published in *The Chamber Magazine*, *Noctivagant Press*, *Aphelion*, *The Write Launch*, and *Liquid Imagination*, and have upcoming publications in *Crow & Cross Keys*, *Carmina Magazine*, *Bards & Sages*, and *Overtly Lit*. A Jersey girl at heart, when Lisa's not writing, she's usually listening to hard rock, bouldering, or sipping amaretto sours. Before she started writing novels, she earned her doctorate in veterinary medicine from Tufts University. Find out more about her at https://lisa.voorhe.es or http://facebook.com/lisavoorheesauthor . Interested in becoming a patron? Find out more about how to support her creative work and receive bonus material at http://www.patreon.com/lisavoorhees.

©
Story: Lisa Voorhees
Art: Theo Ellsworth

*As the ship closed range the object
began to resemble the outline of a body.*

The Curious Case of The USS Arroyo

John Kojak

On the morning of March 18th 2022, the guided missile destroyer USS Arroyo was on patrol nine-hundred miles southwest of the Hawaiian Islands. Inside the Combat Information Center, a young radar operator was sitting at his station staring intently at the luminous-green console screen in front of him when a fast-moving air contact suddenly appeared off the port bow. The radarman bolted upright in his seat and called out into his headset, "Unknown air contact, bearing two-nine-zero."

Captain Paul Plott was in his cabin when he got the call.

"Captain, this is Lieutenant Farley in CIC, we have an unidentified air contact approaching at high speed."

Capt. Plott knew they were sailing well south of all civilian air corridors and shipping lanes. Whatever the radar contact was, it shouldn't have been there. "Bearing and range?'

"Bearing two-nine-zero, range one hundred miles." Farley anxiously replied.

Capt. Plott dropped the phone and rushed out of his cabin and down the ladder to CIC. He flew through the door from the well-lit corridor into the dark, cold nerve-center of the ship, illuminated only by the iridescent radar screens, fire-control panels, and weapons consoles.

"Range?" Capt. Plott asked as he leaned over the shoulder of the young radar operator.

"Thirty-five miles, sir."

"Speed?"

"Twelve hundred knots."

"Jesus Christ, the damn thing is almost on top of us."

"Sorry, sir. It popped up out of nowhere," Lt. Farley blurted back from a nearby station.

"Twenty miles," the radarman said. His eyes focused intently on the rapidly approaching blip on his screen.

"Fire Control, light it up," Capt. Plott ordered.

The fire control operator illuminated the contact with the narrow beam of his tracking radar. "Target locked, captain."

"Farley, set all systems weapons free and standby to fire."

Lt. Farley was the ship's Weapons Officer. He carried a special key that allowed the ship's missiles and guns to be fired. He inserted the key into the weapons control console and turned it ninety degrees to the right. The panel's safety lights turned from red to green. "Weapons free, captain."

Capt. Plott knew that if this contact wasn't real, if it was just glitch in the ship's billion-dollar radar system, his career would be over. "Goddammit, Farley. I better not be shooting at birds."

"Twelve miles," the radarman shouted. Shifting nervously in his seat.

Capt. Plott knew it could be a mistake, but he was out of time. "Fire!"

Lt. Farley pressed the launch button. "Birds away."

The ship shuddered violently as a pair of SM-3 surface-to-air missiles exploded out of their vertical launch tubes and accelerated to Mach Three on their way to intercept the target. It was only a matter of seconds before the three small radar contacts merged into one large jagged blip five miles off the ship's port bow, and then quickly faded.

"Target destroyed, sir," The radarman jubilantly reported. A spontaneous outburst of cheers erupted throughout the room.

Capt. Plott walked over to a nearby comms panel and enabled the ship's intercom. "Men, this is the captain—a few minutes ago CIC picked up an unidentified radar contact heading directly toward our ship at over one thousand miles an hour. It is my duty—our duty—to protect this ship and the lives of everyone on board at all times, so I gave the order to engage and destroy the target. We don't know what it was, or where it came from, so I need everyone to stay at their stations and remain alert."

Capt. Plott turned back to Lt. Farley. "I'm going up to the bridge to begin a search for debris. For your sake, Farley, you better hope we find something . . ."

Capt. Plott directed the ship toward the spot where the missile had intercepted the target. It wasn't long before a lookout spotted something.

"Bridge—Port Lookout," a young seaman called out. "I have an object in the water two thousand yards off the port bow. Capt. Plott walked out onto the port bridgewing and took the binoculars from the lookout. The small white spec stood out like a tic-tac on a turd against the cobalt-blue sea.

As the ship closed range the object began to resemble the outline of a body. Capt. Plott could make out a helmet bobbing on top, attached to a flaccid torso, with worm like appendages floating lazily out from the bottom and sides. He recognized it immediately. It was a flight suit—an empty flight suit.

Commander Stone, the ship's executive officer and second in command, and

Lt. Farley joined Capt. Plott outside on the main deck as the ship's diver brought the object onboard. Once the suit was out of the water, it became clear it wasn't a standard military flight suit. It was a space suit.

The suit was made from a stiff white cloth-like material, and there were several metallic control valves and attachment points on the chest and sides. It looked brand new, but it was obvious that the technology was old.

Exactly how old was revealed by a round patch on the right shoulder of the suit that depicted an outdated capsule-style spacecraft circling above the earth. The image was ringed with Cyrillic writing and there was a date—1960. On the left shoulder was a large red patch emblazoned with a golden hammer and sickle and the letters CCCP.

Capt. Plott turned to Lt. Farley. "Did we just shoot down a piece of Russian space junk?" Anger flared in his eyes as he envisioned what that would do to his career.

"It couldn't have been space debris," Lt. Farley stammered. "The target's course, speed, and altitude were constant."

"How do you explain this then?" Capt. Plott asked, clutching the sea-soaked right sleave of the space suit.

"I-I don't know, Captain," Lt. Farley replied.

Cmdr. Stone saw that the young lieutenant was in trouble and quickly interjected, "Yuri Gagarin was the first man in space, but he didn't go up until '61. Who—or what, were the Soviets sending up in 1960?"

"It doesn't really matter now, does it?" Capt. Plott growled. "I just launched a couple of ten-million-dollar missiles at god-knows-what. If this is all we've got, Admiral Akins is really going to ream my ass. You two see what else you can find out about it. I've got to go down to radio and try to explain this to the brass."

Paul Plott walked back into the interior of the ship and quickly descended a ladder toward the communications center. When he reached the bottom of the ladder, a naked man brushed past him heading aft down the main passageway. The man was white as a sheet and his bones poked out from under his skin like a prisoner in a Nazi concentration camp.

This is all I need, Capt. Plott thought. He called out to the naked man, "Hey shipmate, where the hell do you think you're going?"

The pale man stopped and glared back toward Plott—his eyes blue as burning stars. Paul Plott glared back. This was his ship, and he had had just about as much bullshit as he was going take. He was about to unleash a torrent of expletives toward the man when a couple of enlisted sailors suddenly stepped out into the passageway between them.

"Do you know that guy?" Capt. Plott asked the startled sailors.

"No, sir. I have never seen him before," one of them replied.

"Well, you two escort that idiot down to sickbay. I don't have time for this shit, not today."

The sailors reached out to grab the man by the arm. But as soon as their fingers touched his shimmering white flesh the sailor's bodies exploded like firecrackers—*Blam! Blam!*

Plastering the passageway with blood and entrails and sending one of the men's still pumping heart rolling down the deck toward Paul Plott like a macabre bowling ball.

The naked freak, now clothed in a crimson cloak of gore, continued walking aft and then quickly disappeared down a hatch into the aft-steering compartment.

Capt. Plott heard someone wretching behind him. It was his Chief Boatswains Mate, hurling his breakfast into the medley of blood, guts, and brains splayed up and down the passageway. "Boats, call the bridge. Tell them we have a security breach in aft-steering." The Chief didn't speak, he just nodded his head before retching again.

Capt. Plott rushed toward the aft-steering compartment and peered down the hatch. He knew that if you wanted to disable a ship, any ship, the best place to do it was from aft-steering. The rudder controls were there, and that was also where power from the ship's four gas-turbine engines was transferred to its massive twin propeller shafts. As he watched in horror, the blood-drenched ghoul began tearing apart the solid steel gear housings with his bare hands.

Security Alert! Security Alert! blared over the ship's intercom system. *Security Alert, Aft-Steering Compartment! This is not a drill! Security Alert! Security Alert!*

As the ship's Weapons Officer, Lt. Farley was also in charge of the rapid response team, a group of six heavily armed men whose duty it was to secure the ship in case of a security breach. Farley met the other members of his team at the forward weapons locker. He armed himself with a 9mm Beretta pistol. Two of his men took shotguns, two M16 assault rifles, and the last man grabbed a Vietnam era M79 grenade launcher and a bandoleer of 40mm grenades.

As his team hurried toward the rear of the ship, Farley was shocked at the amount of grisly carnage they encountered along the way. The decks and walls looked like something out of a teenage-slasher movie. When they got close, Farley saw Capt. Plott standing beside the hatch leading down into the aft-steering compartment. He looked like he had aged ten years in the few minutes since they were inspecting the space suite. Farley motioned for his men to hang back as he cautiously approached the captain.

"Captain, what the hell is going on? There's blood and guts everywhere?"

Plott looked over at Farley. "This is going to sound nuts, but some crazy bastard killed two seamen back there. He just reached out and touched them, and—*Blam!*—they exploded. Now he's down in aft-steering ripping the place apart with his bare hands. I don't know if he's on drugs or what."

Lt. Farley peered down the ladder. He could see a tall, boney, bald man covered in blood lifting the heavy, solid brass wheel used to turn the ship's rudder off its pedestal. "Jesus Christ, who is that guy? Is he one of ours?"

"I don't know, but we have to stop him or we'll be sitting ducks for another attack."

Lt. Farley called over the two men armed with M-16's. "There is some nut-job down there who might be armed with explosives. We need to take him out—now!" The men scurried down the ladder into the compartment and opened fire, but the bullets appeared to go right through the naked man's body and began ricocheting around the solid steel walls of the compartment.

Farley ducked behind the hatch to dodge the careening bullets. When he turned back, he saw the ghoulish figure grab the still smoking barrels of both rifles and pull his men towards him. Then, just as the captain had described, their bodies burst like blood filled balloons. The blast showered Farley's face with blood and pieces of flesh. He fell backwards just as one of the men's heads flew past him and out of the hatch like a cannonball.

Lt. Farley used his shirt to wipe the gore out of his eyes and then called over the sailor with the M79 Grenade launcher. "Give me the thumper, and the rest of you guys fall back—you too, Captain." The sailor handed Farley the grenade launcher and the bandoleer of ammunition and then retreated back down the passageway with the others.

Lt. Farley flipped open the barrel of the M79 and inserted one of the large grenade cartridges. "You're gonna get it now, you albino son of a bitch." He pointed the barrel down through the open hatch, leaned back, and pulled the trigger. *Boom!* The quarter-inch steel walls of the small compartment magnified the intensity of the blast from the two-and-a-half-pound shell, making the entire ship tremble. He fired his grenades again and again, until he was sure that nothing, not even the devil himself, could be alive down there.

After the last round was spent, Farley peered down into what was left of the compartment. There were small fires burning everywhere and a thick layer of dark acrid smoke filled the air. The floor and walls were covered in blood and mangled body parts, but the freakish fiend was gone.

Capt. Plott creeped back toward Farley. "Is he dead?"

"Nothing is alive down there, I'm sure of that."

Capt. Plott looked down into the destroyed compartment. "I'm going to the radio room. Get the Chief Engineer to send a team to put out these fires and see if we can restore power to the shafts, then take the rest of your men and sweep the boat. I don't want any more surprises."

Lt. Duncan's jaw hit the floor when he saw Capt. Plott enter the communications center. Paul Plott's face looked like his skin had detached from the bones and his uniform was spattered with blood and what looked like little pieces of raw meat.

"Get me a secure channel to CINCPAC Fleet," Plott barked at the startled communications officer.

"I'm sorry, sir, SATCOMMS are down."

"What?!? Why wasn't I notified?"

"They just went down, sir. Everything is down. We can't transmit or receive on any frequencies."

"Dammit, Duncan. Our steering and propulsion systems have been wrecked, and for all I know we could come under attack again any minute. I need comms—not excuses. I'm heading up to the bridge; I want to know as soon as comms are up."

When Capt. Plott reached the bridge, Cmdr. Stone was waiting for him with a walkie-talkie in his hand. "The Chief engineer reports that the fires are out, but the main reduction gears are too damaged to repair, sir. We are effectively dead in the water."

"Great . . . I expected as much. Has Farley reported in?"

As if on cue, Lt. Farley's voice crackled over the intercom. "Bridge—Farley. We completed our sweep. The ship's clear, sir."

"Good work, Farley. Report back to CIC. I will call you if I need you." Capt. Plott climbed up into the oversized, leather captain's chair that provided a panoramic view of the bridge and sea around them. He leaned back and ran his fingers through his rapidly thinning hair. That was something at least, he thought. It was about time he caught a break.

Cmdr. Stone leaned in towards the captain and spoke softly so the rest of the bridge team wouldn't hear. "I heard the guy who tried to sabotage the ship—I heard he was naked—do you think that might have had something to do with the empty space suit we found? Do you think it might have been his?"

"Do I think the saboteur was an elderly Russian astronaut, who somehow returned to the earth sixty years later, to attack our ship—in the nude?" Plott's eyes glared at his XO with unconcealed contempt.

"You never know." Cmdr. Stone stammered. "The Soviets did a lot of crazy stuff. Maybe they sent the crew up with a cryochamber, or they might have even been playing around with some type of time travel or teleportation experiments—like we did in Philadelphia during World War II."

"You believe that crap . . . " It was more a declaration of Stone's stupidity than a question.

"All I'm saying is that stranger things have happened, Paul. Look at those mysterious disks our pilots encountered off San Diego. They flew circles around our fighters, and then dove down thirty-thousand feet and disappeared under the water in a matter of seconds. That wasn't the first encounter either . . . I remember hearing that Neil Armstrong and Buzz Aldrin reported seeing weird lights following their Apollo 11 capsule—maybe the Russians did too, we just never heard about it. Hell, for all we know the crew of that Soviet spaceship might have been abducted."

"By what—aliens?" Capt. Plott scowled. It took every ounce of self-control he could muster not to reach over and strangle Stone on the spot.

Paul Plott was imagining his fingers wrapping tightly around his Stone's neck when the bridge telephone began to ring. Stone answered and meekly handed the handset to the captain. "It's Duncan, sir."

"Tell me we have comms, Lieutenant."

"Well, not exactly, sir. We still can't transmit or receive on any of our standard frequencies. But, on a hunch, I scanned some amateur radio bands and was able to detect some faint CW traffic."

"CW?"

"Continuous Wave, sir. HAM radio operators still use it to send Morse code. I thought if we are able to receive CW through the interference, we might be able to transmit on it

as well."

"Lieutenant, we are almost a thousand mile from the nearest naval base. How the hell do you expect us to communicate with anyone using shortwave radio?"

"There is an old HAM radio operator technique called moonbounce . . . If we can direct a powerful enough shortwave transmission to-wards the moon, we can bounce the signal off the surface back toward the earth. I ran some calculations; at our present angle the signal should reflect down somewhere over the North-western United States. There are hundreds of amateur radio operators who monitor those frequencies, someone should pick up our signal and alert the fleet."

"Moonbounce? You sound crazier than Mulder over here," Capt. Plott glared at Stone.

"Um, I know how it sounds, captain, but I grew up around these guys, my uncle was a HAM radio operator. I think it could work."

"What the hell . . . it makes about as much sense as everything else that's hap-pened today. How long is it going to take you to set up?

"I have already re-aligned

the antennas, sir. Everything is ready to go."

Capt. Plott walked over to the navigation table to check the ships position. He gave Lt. Duncan the coordinates and told him to send out the SOS. He knew that even if this ridiculous plan worked and the message somehow got through, there was no way the brass was going to believe it. Hell, he didn't believe it.

He climbed back in his chair and tried to prepare himself for what might happen next. He was starting to hope that the worst may be over when the port lookout suddenly shouted out, "Contact dead ahead, two miles."

Capt. Plott looked out over the bow of the ship and could see a huge, metallic silver disk slowly emerging out of the sea. Enormous sheets of water cascaded down along its face as it rose slowly above the waves and began to hover a few hundred feet above the surface. The disk was the size of a ten-story building.

"I knew it. It's the goddamn aliens," Cmdr. Stone muttered. He looked too terrified to be afraid.

Capt. Plott watched in silence as the enormous disk began to rotate on its axis, like a spinning coin, increasing in speed until the water underneath it churned violently into a large swirling vortex. Every hair on his body was standing at attention. "I don't know what that is—but it's going to suck us down to the bottom if we don't destroy it."

Capt. Plott reached over and turned on the intercom to CIC. "Combat—Bridge, we have a large object hovering just above the surface two miles off our bow. Lock the fire control radars on target and standby to fire."

"Fire what, sir?" Lt. Farley asked.

"Everything . . ."

Capt. Plott stood stoically on the bridge as the Arroyo released a furious barrage on the alien object. The deck beneath his feet shuddered as dozens of supersonic missiles flew out of their launch tubes, *Whomf! Whomf! Whomf!* and screamed toward their target. After the missile silos were empty, the ship's rapid fire five-inch gun spit out its high explosive shells *Ka-Boom! Ka-Boom! Ka-Boom!* But the weapons had no effect on the strange craft. After a few minutes the guns fell silent, and with no ability to maneuver or communicate, the once mighty warship was helpless. All the sailors on the bridge could do was watch as the huge disk continued to spin faster and faster, pulling the destroyer reluctantly forward until the Arroyo's bow slowly tipped over into the swirling vortex, and the ship was sucked down into the unforgiving sea.

Epilogue

The last known communication received from the USS Arroyo was in the form of a strange, unencrypted SOS message that was passed along to the United States Navy by an amateur HAM radio operator in Oregon. The message gave a set of latitude and longitude coordinates and read simply, "Attacked by unknown forces." The message, and the way it was received, made no sense to Adm. Jim Akins, The Commander of the U.S. Pacific Fleet. After attempts to contact the Arroyo failed, he launched one of the largest search and rescue operations in naval history. For three days and three nights, fourteen ships and over two-dozen aircraft searched hundreds of square miles of ocean. One of the search ships reported finding an old Soviet style flight suite floating in the water near the USS Arroyo's last reported position, but no trace of the ship or her crew were ever found.

©
Story: John Kojak
Art: Darren Auck

John Kojak *is a United States Navy Veteran and graduate of The University of Texas who grew up in oily little towns around Houston, Texas during the Boom-and-Bust eras of the 1970s and '80s. He still lives there, with a nice woman and a mean cat. His poetry and short stories have appeared in a variety of books and magazines such as Poetry Quarterly, The American Journal of Poetry, California's Best Emerging Poets, Chronogram Magazine, Mystery Weekly, Switchblade Magazine, Pulp Modern, and many others.*

Dark Amplifications:
The Edgar Allan Poe Adaptations of Richard Corben

Anthony Perconti

On December 2nd, 2020 American illustrator par excellence Richard Corben passed from this mortal coil. As a teenager with a preoccupation with comic books and comic culture, growing up in the United States in the late 1980s and 1990s, Corben's shadow loomed large. I was first exposed to his work incidentally through the "Den" section of the 1981 cult classic film, *Heavy Metal* Corben's work certainly had a unique resonance to it. "Den" (masterfully voiced by the incomparable John Candy) was an unabashed adolescent male power fantasy, full of impossible physiques (both male and female), fell sorcery, sex and violence ratcheted up to eleven, with the knob broken off and on amphetamines. Subtle, it certainly wasn't. Den was instantly recognizable, what with his bald pate and Schwarzenegger like physique. I encountered his further adventures in the pages of (naturally enough)

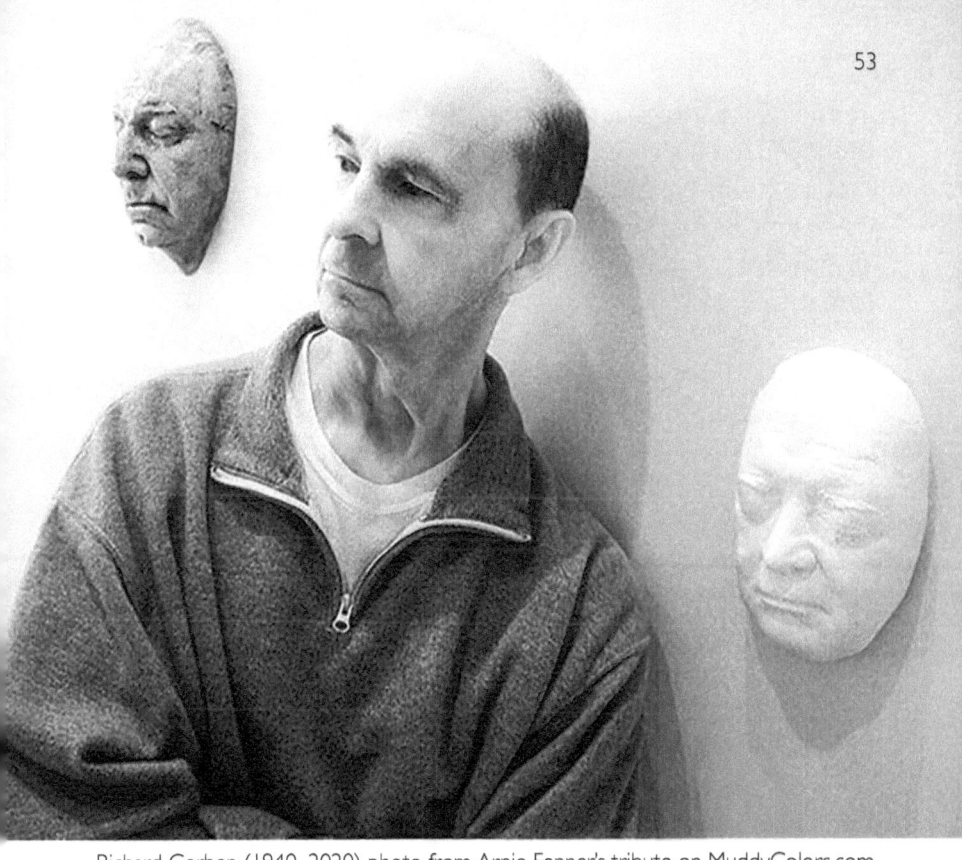

Richard Corben (1940–2020) photo from Arnie Fenner's tribute on MuddyColors.com

the European influenced *Heavy Metal Magazine* (or *Metal Hurlant* for you Francophiles out there). Issue number one hundred and forty-one, with a Simon Bisley cover, if I recall correctly. Corben's distinct visual style (much like the aforementioned, Simon Bisley), was easy as pie to pick out on the magazine racks and in the back issue long boxes. I soon learned that Richard Corben had a successful and consistent career as an illustrator, prior to his muscle-bound character showing up in that animated feature. A career that stretches back to the American "Underground Comix" movement of the late 1960s. Corben's name was in the same orbit with creators such as Spain Rodriguez, Tom Veitch and Mike Vosburg, to say nothing of his robust Warren Publishing output throughout the 1970s. When I think of Corben's visuals, certain descriptors come easily to mind: muscular, alien, horrifying, fantastic. But gothic? Not necessarily. Yet, this is indeed the case. The fact that he could "go gothic" is a credit to the man's versatility as an artist and his lifelong commitment to the mastery of his craft. In addition to all of his signature works of lurid underground horror and psychedelic fantasy (and there are many), Richard Corben also translated many of Edgar Allan Poe's writings into the comics medium. That Nineteenth Century American practitioner of the macabre short tale (and poem) found the perfect steward of his oeuvre, one hundred and some odd years after his death in a counterculture comics artist hailing from Anderson, Missouri. Or as Dr. M. Thomas Inge states: "Corben may well be our most acute and creative interpreter of Poe in visual terms. All of his comic book work has been imbued with the same gothic sensibilities and keen eye for the grotesque that possessed Poe himself."[1]

Edgar Allan Poe's writing career ranged from 1827 to 1849. In that time, he left an indelible mark in American (and I would venture to say, World) Literature. Poe was responsible for many of the conventions that are so commonplace to readers today. Although he decidedly *did not* invent the gothic tale, his stories and poems in this mode increased the popularity of the form, to a much greater degree. Take for example, how many generations of school children are (at least, passingly) familiar with his most famous piece of verse, "The Raven." Stories such as "The Gold Bug" and the C. Auguste Dupin trilogy laid the groundwork for the modern detective story as we know it. These tales are considered so foundational, that the Mystery Writers of America honor their best and brightest with the award commonly known as "The Edgar", a shortened version of the Edgar Allan Poe Award. A through line can be drawn directly to that world famous English consulting detective Sherlock Holmes, from his Parisian antecedent, that master of 'ratiocination', Dupin. Both are brilliant thinking machines whose deductive powers seem to border on the supernatural,

Right: *The Raven and the Red Death* No. 0 cover art (2013) Dark Horse.

when viewed by mere mortals. In addition to his contributions to the mystery genre, Poe had an integral part in creating the type of story known as the *conte cruel*. "The *conte cruel* is, as *The A to Z of Fantasy Literature* by Brian Stableford states, a "short-story genre that takes its name from an 1883 collection by Villiers de l'Isle Adam, although previous examples had been provided by such writers as Edgar Allan Poe. Some critics use the label to refer only to non-supernatural horror stories, especially those that have nasty climactic twists, but it is applicable to any story whose conclusion exploits the cruel aspects of the 'irony of fate.'"[2] These "nasty climatic twists" and cruel, ironic endings are an intrinsic aspect of Poe's fiction. That is why they are so exhilarating, exciting and I would contend, timeless. Once you read a Poe story or two and become familiar with his distinct style, *you just know* that things are not going to end well—that one way or another, doom is on the way. Poe's psychological horror stories, these little *conte cruels*, are as entertaining today, as they were when they were first published in the first half of the Nineteenth Century.

In 1846, Poe's treatise "The Philosophy of Composition" stated that fiction should create what he called a "unity of effect". "Poe's primary concern was "unity of effect," which means that every element of a story should help create a single emotional impact."[3]

Tone, theme, characters, setting and plot should all work in concert and in service to a singular vision. Or to state it differently, these components should build to the big payoff at the tale's conclusion. Poe's take on writing fiction was that of a watchmaker: the parts are in service of the greater (singular) whole. The knockout punch is finally delivered in the twelfth round and the reader is left reeling and stupefied at what they just read: this is Poe's bread and butter time and time again. This technique of "unity of effect" was also adopted by the Twentieth Century illustrator, Richard Corben. Especially as it pertains to his visual representations of Poe's work

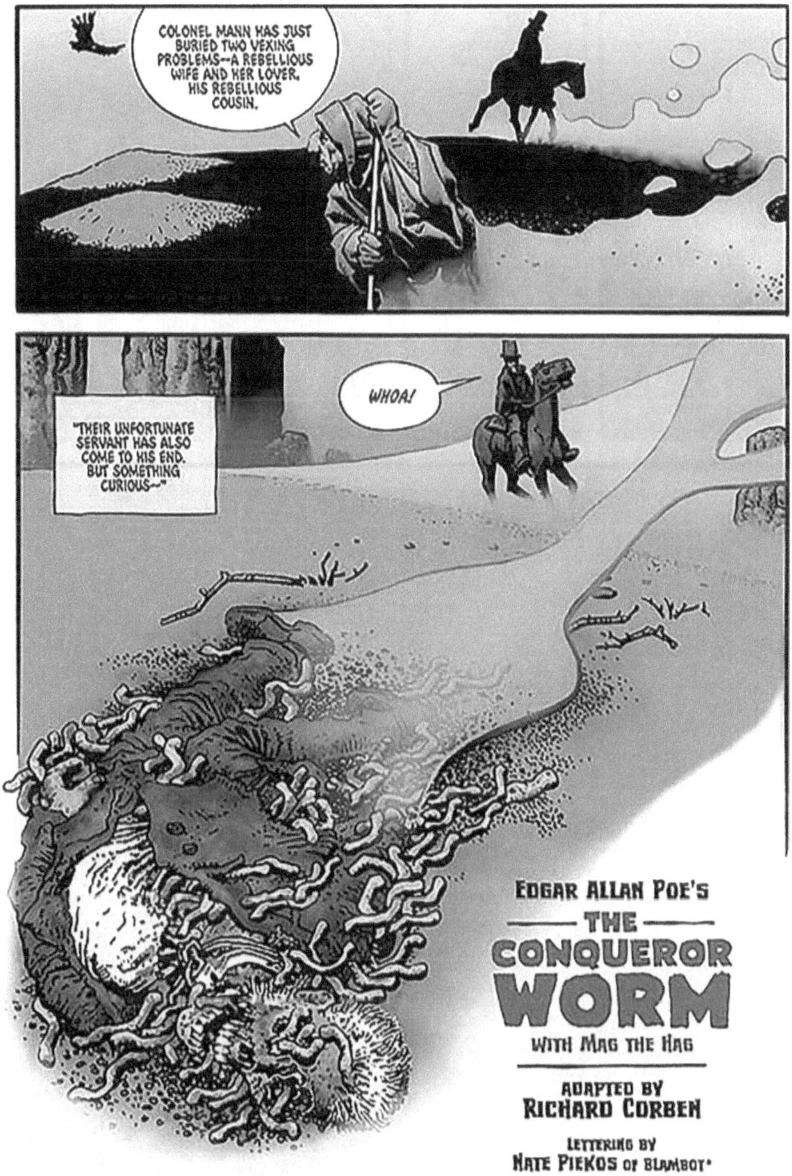

Splash page from *The Conqueror Worm* No. 0 (2012) Dark Horse.

in the medium of comic books. Corben's early adaptations of Poe were quite literal. Take his 1974 collaboration with writer Richard Margopolous, for example. This version of "The Raven" appeared in Warren Publishing's *Creepy*, number

Page 2 from *The Conqueror Worm* No. 0 (2012) Dark Horse.

sixty-seven and is a quite conventional (yet excellent) retelling of the famous poem. The same could be said of the 1975 adaptation (albeit with a few flourishes) of Poe's story, "The Oval Portrait" in *Creepy* number sixty-nine. These translations are rife with mood and atmosphere: a consistent touchstone of Corben's unique art style. They have that gothic touch, through and through. But it is his later Poe works that are much more interesting and innovative (in my view), while still retaining that all important "unity of effect."

In a 2012 interview with *The Comics Journal*, Richard Corben stated that: "My first intent was to do so-called faithful adaptations. But now I feel a "faithful" adaptation is not possible in any medium by anybody. My early impressions of Poe's work came from Roger Corman's/ Richard Matheson's versions of some Poe stories. Other than the titles, these films have very little to do with Poe's stories. After thinking about other possible directions, they might have taken, other possible amplifications, they all represent a departure from the original intent. However, this certainly won't stop countless writers and artists (and me) from doing their own take on Poe's stories. So, resolved not to do "faithful" adaptations, I am freed to let the inspiration flow. Yes, the stories and poems are "springboards" for my interpretations."[4] In a fascinating and seemingly paradoxical twist of fate, once Corben began utilizing Poe's works as creative "springboards" did his ever important "unity of effect" become further amplified. To this end, his 2006 three issue Marvel Max series (and subsequent collection), *Haunt of Horror: Edgar Allan Poe* was a departure from "faithful" adaptations. The series adapted two of Poe's stories and eight poems. "Israfel" was changed to the spelling "Izrafel" and set in the modern day, with a hip-hop artist's tragic killing due to gangland rivalries. While "The Conqueror Worm" was transposed to a bleak post-apocalyptic world, where animal life has all but perished. To say nothing of the *second* (and not the final)

Spirits of the Dead 2nd edition (2019) Dark Horse trade paperback, 216 pages.

2014's *Spirits of the Dead* (Dark Horse Books). I am of the opinion that the adaptations presented in this collection are Corben's finest tribute to Edgar Allan Poe. They are his definitive statement on the subject and the man. Although, I suspect that if Corben was still with us today, he would no doubt continue his exercise in Poe permutations. "After a period of time I usually come back with some new thought or interpretation," Corben said. "I think it's because he deals with subjects with a universal appeal."[5] *Spirits* consists of adaptations of nine tales and five poems. Each and every one of them is suffused with a sense of grim foreboding and inescapable doom. The auteur embeds the poem "The Haunted Palace"

iteration of "The Raven." Like a jazz virtuoso or a classical musician riffing on a familiar tune, Corben was drawing inspiration from the well and putting another twist on the source material.

Yet for all its stylized storytelling and inventiveness, I would contend that *Haunt of Horror* pales in comparison to

Madeline Usher from *The Fall of the House of Usher* No. 1 (2013) Dark Horse.

within his reworking on "The Masque of the Red Death" and it works absolutely perfectly in this context. His longest interpretation (that clocks in at forty-seven pages in length) is his masterful take on "The Fall of the House of Usher," while blending elements of "The Oval Portrait '' into the narrative structure. Corben more than implies that the relationship between sister and brother, Madeline and Roderick is not exactly traditional. The poem "The

"The City in the Sea" splash page from *Spirits of the Dead* (2014) Dark Horse.

"The City in the Sea" select panels from page 2 of *Spirits of the Dead* (2014) Dark Horse.

City in the Sea" is used as the basis to convey a tale of divine or perhaps more accurately, infernal judgment and retribution. The artist for all intents and purposes, *covers his own* Poe covers yet again. Not content with a second rendition of "The Raven," Corben treats readers to yet a third macabre version. "The Conqueror Worm " (last seen in *Haunt of Horror*) is translated into a weird western tale, containing a bizarre Theater of Dreams, disquieting puppets and a highly rapacious species of parasitic worm. Corben fleshes out and adds some interesting flourishes to the first (and most well-known)

Dupin tale, "The Murders in the Rue Morgue" as well. Rounding out this volume is Corben's coda on one of Poe's most enduring tales, "The Cask of Amontillado." *In pace requiescat*, indeed. Aiding and abetting on the aesthetics of *Spirits* are Beth Corben Reed (Richard's daughter) on coloring duties and letterer, Nate Piekos. In contrast, *Haunt of Horror* was produced in black and white. Reed and Piekos' contributions to this collection are exquisite. The colors pop off the page and Piekos' wide ranging lettering talents add to the ever important "unity of effect" heralded by Poe: these two contributors add much to the overall atmosphere of the stories. "Everything in a Corben page is functional and there are no empty artistic gestures to fill space."[6]

Richard Corben paid homage to EC Comics' The Crypt-Keeper and DC's Cain and Abel (from *House of Mystery*) in both *Haunt of Horror: Edgar Allan Poe* and *Spirits of the Dead* with Uncle Deadgar and Mag the Hag, respectively. These two characters at times interact within the narrative structures (especially Mag) of the stories, while regularly breaking the Fourth Wall, usually at the beginning or at the conclusion of a tale. They address us, the readers with a sly quip and knowing wink at the typically horrible fates visited upon the players of these *conte cruels*. Mag and Uncle Deadgar, like their precursors from *The Vault of Horror*, *The Haunt of Fear* and *House of Mystery* act as the Greek Chorus in a tragedy, commenting on the lurid spectacle and folly of mankind. And while Poe's (and by extension, Corben's) *contes* are unequivocally *cruel*, they all contain a strong element of morality. These

grisly little morality plays give the reader a sensationalistic shock, to be sure. But more often than not, the reader is also privy to the *consequences* of the crime or transgression: sooner or later, the wheel turns and the bill comes due. Or if you like, what comes around, goes around. To stretch the EC analogy a bit further, the works showcased in *Haunt of Horror* and *Spirits of the Dead* have traditional William Gaines-like denouements. Gruesome and poetic justice is doled out in large helpings, oftentimes from beyond the grave. Publisher Gaines was certainly one to mine the works of Poe (among others writers) for ideas to fuel his EC line of horror-themed comics. How could you blame him? Poe was an absolute master of the short story form. Readers familiar with George A. Romero's 1982 feature, *Creepshow* should feel right at home with these two Poe collections.

In my view, Richard Corben's *Haunt of Horror* and (especially) *Spirits of the Dead* deserve a place on every discriminating Edgar Allan Poe fan's bookshelf (right next to his *The Complete Tales and Poems*). Corben's unique art style was the perfect complement to the gothic and macabre sensibilities of Poe. The artist had the innate ability to re-examine Poe's works and create haunting new variations of them, all the while respecting the author's original vision of the source material. The Poe-Corben collaboration is a gift to fans of literature and comic books, alike. Once again, Dr. Inge: "Thus his alliance with Poe has been a fortuitous and productive one. It is a marriage made in . . . well, one hesitates to say *heaven*. Time and again Corben has turned, or returned, to his favorite poems and stories, each demonstrating an original vision, a new way to interpret or understand Poe's themes."[7] But enough of my yammering. Turn that page and enjoy the dark majesty that is the haunting collaboration between Edgar Allan Poe and his Twentieth Century steward, Richard Corben.

Notes

1. Corben, Richard. *Edgar Allan Poe's Spirits of the Dead*. Dark Horse Books. Second Edition, 2019.
2. https://philslattery.org/what-is-horror/the-lexicon-of-horror/
3. https://dariusjoneswriter.com/2014/01/24/the-craft-poes-unity-of-effect/#:~:text=Poe's%20primary%20concern%20was%20%E2%80%9Cunity,create%20a%20single%20emotional%20impact.
4. https://www.tcj.com/and-to-have-more-control-i-would-have-to-do-more-richard-corben-on-adapting-ed-gar-allan-poe/
5. https://richmond.com/graphic-view-of-poe/article_8e8d1ac6-bd93-50a3-bd02-1c3c2473a043.html
6. Corben, Richard. *Edgar Allan Poe's Spirits of the Dead*. Dark Horse Books. Second Edition, 2019.
7. Corben, Richard. *Edgar Allan Poe's Spirits of the Dead*. *Dark* Horse Books. Second Edition, 2019.

Article: Anthony Perconti

Anthony Perconti lives and works in the hinterlands of New Jersey with his wife and kids. He enjoys well-crafted and engaging stories across a variety of genres and mediums. His articles have appeared in several online venues and can be found on Twitter at @AnthonyPerconti.

Fantagor No. 1 (1971 second printing) Last Gasp.

Death Rattle No. 1 (1972) Kitchen Sink.

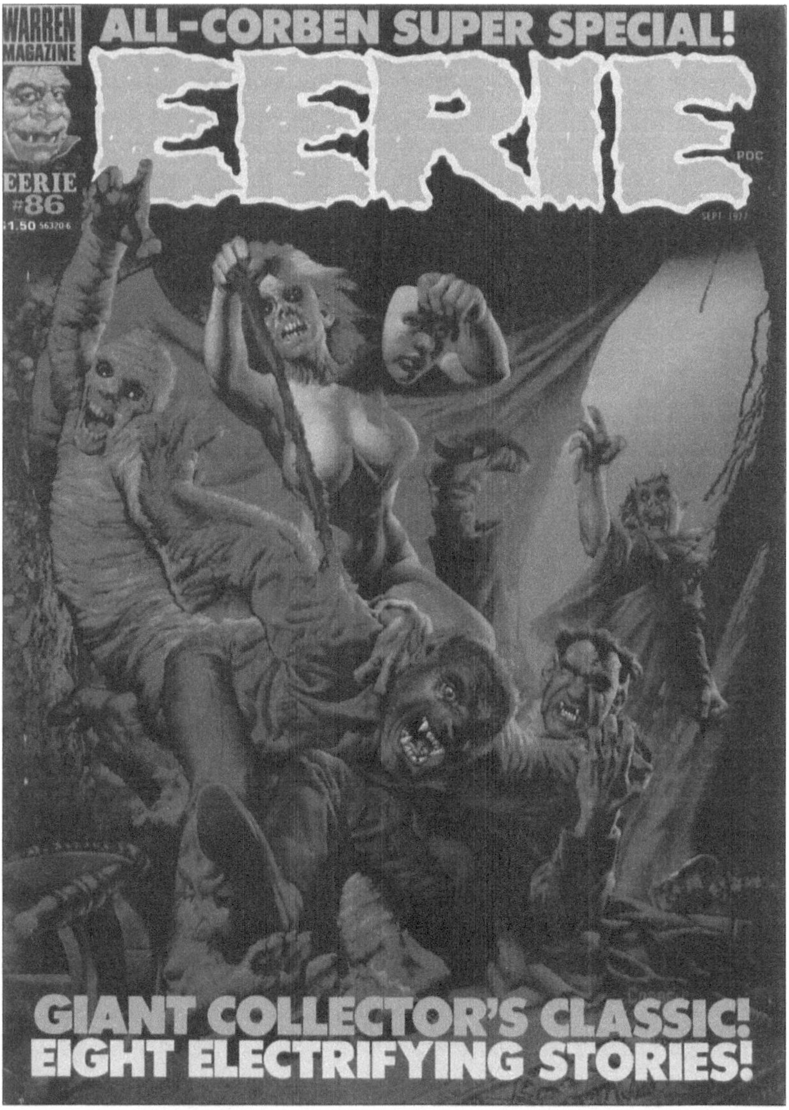

Eerie No. 86 (1977) Warren Magazines.

Hot Stuf' No. 5 (1977) Sal Q. Productions.

"Izrafel" page from *Haunt of Horror* No. 3 (2006) Marvel Comics.

Premature Burial No. 1 cover art (2014) Dark Horse.

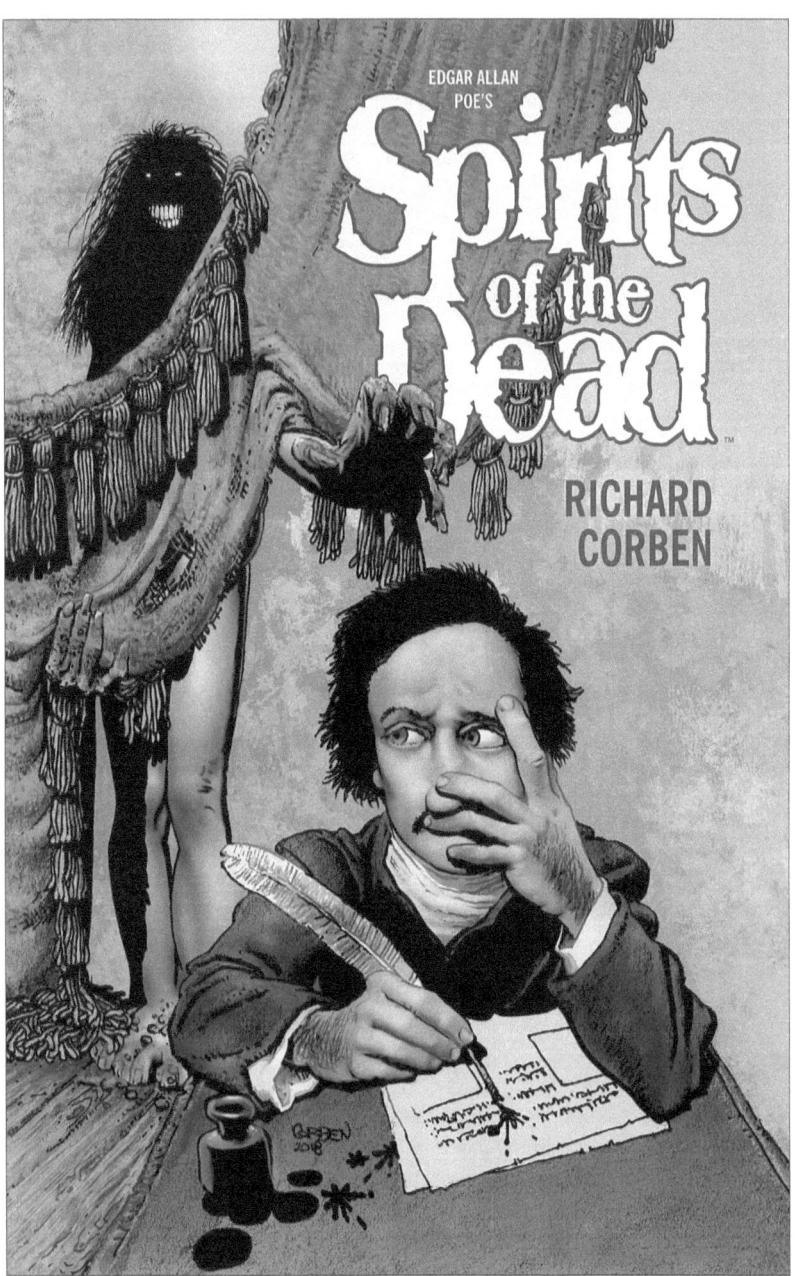

Spirits of the Dead 1st edition (2014) Dark Horse hardcover, 216 pages.

Morelia and Murders in the Rue Morgue No. 0 cover art (2014) Dark Horse.

He wasn't harassing or threatening anybody. There weren't any laws against dressing like a clown in public.

10-48

Sarah Cannavo

"You know, Nate, I'm starting to think you had the right idea," Sam Pert said, brown eyes drifting across the dark road beyond the parked patrol car's windshield. "Settling down, high school sweetheart, all that crap. Coulda saved me a lot of trouble."

"Yeah, but it wasn't that hard a decision for me," Nate Browne pointed out, grinning. "I only had the one sweetheart."

Sam chuckled, crumpling his gum wrapper, the scent of cinnamon heating the inside of Car 22. "True, true."

"Besides, Tania's a good girl," Nate continued. "Good for you. I've seen it."

"No, I know." Sam ran a hand through his thick dark hair. "I'm not saying anything against her. It's just that I probably made things a helluva lot harder than they had to be up 'til now."

"So it took you a little longer to get there. What matters is you made it eventually." His partner's shrug was paternal; his attitude toward Sam often was, despite the single year's difference between them.

"All right, stop that."

"What?"

"Being so rational. It irritates me."

Nate raised his hands, wedding band glinting in a sheen of moonlight. "Sorry, Officer. Don't shoot."

Sam winged the ball of silver foil at Nate with a pitcher's precision. It bounced off his shoulder and disappeared into the car's dark while Nate laughed. Outside the still night air simmered on. Beneath their voices, the radio's static drone competed with the insects chorusing out in the brush—no calls, though, to rescue Car 22 from the monotony of

Friday-night speed-trap duty.

Sam settled back in the passenger seat and sighed. "Maybe you remember who it was."

Nate turned blue eyes on him. "Who what was?"

"Who the hell we pissed off to get stuck with this shit."

"It was our turn in the rotation, Sam."

Sam mock-glared. "You're doing it again."

It was a July Friday night, which meant most of Sutton, Ohio's younger generation would be at Woodward Lake, swimming, partying, and making mildly to severely bad decisions. *That* meant some of Sutton's Finest were posted on the desolate stretch of highway heading to and from the lake to watch for drunk drivers or speeders. Watch and wait. Nobody on the force's favorite post—for good reason, Nate thought. He understood Sam's frustration. In the three hours they'd been sitting here the only movement had been a car driving the speed limit and straight as an arrow back toward town, and a deer darting from the trees and across the blacktop, leading Sam to complain he was hungry.

Nate would've rather been back at the air-conditioned station, and more than that at home with Jessie and the kids. He also knew exactly where Sam would rather be, and what he'd be doing. But if they really wanted excitement, they wouldn't have stayed in Sutton, where the worst crimes were typically drunk-and-disorderlies or domestic disturbances, and the general day-to-day array of offenses ran far below that. And, most importantly, a quiet patrol meant another safe night. Nate suspected applying this logic wouldn't improve Sam's mood any, so instead he said, "I seem to remember a few keggers up at Woodward Lake in our own youth."

"Yeah, but we were never dumb enough to drive home afterward." Sam shifted restlessly in his seat.

"Fair enough," Nate relented.

Half an hour passed to the chirping of crickets and the crackle of static, the sounds of a slow night in Sutton. Eleven o'clock drew nearer, and Sam was about to duck into the bushes for a bathroom break when Winnie Scott's voice spilled into the car, shattering the stillness.

"We've got a 10-48 in the vicinity of Sutton Woods, by the Kinney Road turnoff. I repeat, a 10-48. Car 22, you're closest, please respond."

10-48: a suspicious person. *That* was a rare call in a town where everyone knew everybody else in a near-claustrophobic closeness. Nate couldn't remember the last time it'd gone out. He turned the car on and picked up the radio while Sam whooped and slapped the roof. "This is Car 22, Dispatch," Nate said with a patient glance at his partner. "Heading out there now. What's the nature of the call?"

Silence. Nate and Sam shared a look. Nate clicked the radio again. "Winnie? Winnie, you there? What's going on?"

"Caller reported—well, the caller reported a clown in the woods."

Nate stared at the radio. Sam started, "What the f—"

"Winnie, are you screwing with us?" Nate asked, though he knew she wasn't. She had a healthy sense of humor, but when it came to work she never messed around.

"Of course not. I'm just as confused as you are."

"Who called it in?" Sam was glad Nate was asking the questions. All he could seem to do was keep mouthing *"Clown?"*

"Larry Haskell. Said he was driving home and saw a clown at the edge of the woods, just standing there staring."

Well, that put things into perspective. If Larry Haskell was seeing random clowns in the woods, he'd either been drinking again or had just stopped drinking again. "All right, Dispatch," Nate said. "Sam and I are heading over now—and tell you what, after we check things out we'll stop by Larry's and check on him, too, make sure everything's okay."

"Roger, Car 22."

"Bit weird even for Larry Haskell," Sam observed as they pulled onto the road, heading east toward Kinney. "Even if he's been drinking his cousin from Georgia's backyard brew—which I've never, ever tried, of course."

"Of course," Nate said dryly. "And yeah, it is, but it's still more plausible than an actual clown hanging out in Sutton Woods at eleven at night."

Sam shook his head. "I reiterate, who the hell'd we piss off to get stuck with this shit?"

It was barely five minutes to Kinney Road. As they neared Nate slowed the car to a cruise so they could scan the jagged black line of the woods, not expecting much. They were still talking easily, discussing potential presents for Tania's birthday. When their headlights' yellow beams swept the trees near the turnoff, both men fell silent, staring.

Because there stood the clown.

Yellow suit, gloves white as its painted face, oversized shoes, nose and greasepaint smile all the same vivid scarlet—just standing, just staring, just as Larry had said. Had it not moved at all? It didn't move now, even as the headlights pinned it to the trees, the car drawing to a stop and the cops within staring back, it didn't move and didn't speak.

"Uh, buddy?" Sam said, enthusiasm at having a call

doused by disbelief. "You seeing this, too?"

"Apparently."

"I thought that'd make me feel better." Sam paused. "It doesn't."

Nate rubbed his stubbled jaw. "So I guess we should . . ."

"Yeah, probably."

The two men exited the car. The hot air felt thicker now, harder to breathe, as if swelling like cotton batting in their lungs, with an electric crackling to it, something that made the hair on the back of Sam's neck prickle. It was the tension of approaching the unknown, of not knowing who or what you were facing or what they might decide to do, and it was in no way diminished by this figure's arc of kinky red hair or the puffy buttons descending the front of its baggy suit. When they told this story back at the station the other guys might laugh—he and Nate would definitely be finding balloon animals on their desks for weeks to come—but there was nothing funny now about the circus escapee standing there, silent and so chillingly still.

"Sir?" Nate's voice was level, calm, as he and Sam

slowly approached. "Sir, we're with the Sutton police. We've received some complaints about you."

Sam waited for it; the woods and roads were public property, so he wasn't technically trespassing. He wasn't harassing or threatening anybody. There weren't any laws against dressing like a clown in public.

Nothing. The clown stayed quiet, crimson grin glistening in the moonlight. Sam's hackles rose. His right hand drifted nearer to the gun at his waist, Nate mirroring the movement beside him.

Weird, this whole damn thing is just too fucking weird . . .

"Sir," Nate said again. "If you've got any ID on you I'd like you to slowly get it out for me, okay?"

The clown repeated its non-response, and the sense of alien wrongness grew, running under Sam's skin, itching and burning down to the bone. A glance at his partner told him it was crawling through Nate too.

"Sir," Sam said, voice a harsher bark than Nate's had been. "Do you understand what we're telling you?"

They were close enough now to see the real mouth the painted one ringed. It was set in a line that betrayed nothing, no intention, no flicker of emotion, and not a single syllable. The clown's eyes, its entire expression, were a void, utterly empty, emotionless; it might've been a mask, except Sam could see faint creases in the greasepaint, the texture of flesh beneath the smooth white façade. A hollow yawned wide in Sam's stomach and his heart hammered his ribs, adrenaline flooding his blood. He'd never responded to anything the way he was responding to this thing—*thing*, yes. He realized he'd never thought of this clown as anything but an "it," something in him refusing instinctively from the start to recognize it as a fellow man. What it actually *was*, though . . .

"All right, I need you to raise your hands—*slowly*—and put them behind your head," Nate said. "We'll see if we can't get this sorted out down at the station."

The clown followed this order as well as it had the others. Not a stir—and the men noticed the sluggish breeze blowing hot and damp through the trees didn't seem to touch the clown's spray of hair or baggy suit. All at once Sam realized the crickets had stopped chirping, the silence further rubbing his frayed nerves raw.

"All right, that's it," he said, jaw set, some taut thread snapping in him. Striding forward he reached for the clown, but his hand closed on empty air instead of its wrist as the figure disappeared, winking out quick as an extinguished light.

"What the—" Sam whipped around. "Nate, where'd the bastard g—"

As Nate watched, it popped into sight at Sam's back. "Behind you!" he called, drawing his gun. Just as Sam turned the clown jumped him, slamming him to the ground.

Spots danced in Sam's eyes. He grunted wordlessly as impact drove the air from his lungs. The body atop his was weightier than even a full-grown man's should've been, and though he struggled against the press the blows he landed weren't having the desired effect. His attacker, however, had no such problems.

"Nate," he forced out, "a little goddamn *help*?"

Nate couldn't get a clear bead; the pair in the dirt were moving too much. A bullet had just as much a chance of piercing his partner as his assailant. So, thinking dimly of high school fights, and loudly that this couldn't possibly be happening, Nate waded into the fray, fists bunching in the back of the clown's suit.

"Stand down!" he snarled, yanking hard.

The clown didn't cling to Sam, or fly back off-balance. It vanished again, leaving Nate reeling and Sam sprawled out, battered and dirt-streaked.

"You all right?" Nate asked.

"Fucking-A," Sam growled, ignoring Nate's proffered hand and shoving himself to his feet, teeth gritted against his body's protests.

"Come on," Nate said, ordering his whirling thoughts with procedure, what had to be done. He'd let the rest of it in later, after this had been dealt with. "We'll go back to the car, radio this i—"

There. Six feet behind Nate. Sam rushed past him, anger exacerbated by the throbbing where the blows had struck and the fear this fucker had made him feel. He barely heard Nate calling out as he sprinted by.

But as he neared the clown he *did* hear, over the blood pounding in his ears, some low, indistinct hum, a buzz around the figure like a babble of distant voices, overlapping and unintelligible. The sound made Sam's skin crawl. It was as if he was catching some snatch of chatter coming through a tear in the night air, maybe the same kind this figure kept slipping through.

What is *this thing?*

It felt solid enough as Sam slammed into it; he seemed to grip flesh and bone as he bent the clown's arm behind its back, clipping a cuff around its left wrist. "You have the right to remain silent." *No kidding.* "Anything you s—"

The cuffs dropped to the ground. Before Sam could react, the clown had its gloved hands around his throat and was squeezing, lifting him. His boots wheeled in midair, black spots bursting in his vision, an inhuman chill seeping from beneath the slick silk gloves to infect his skin. The clown's red grin seemed more like a leer now, looming beneath him as he thrashed in the strangling grasp and gasped for air that wouldn't come.

A shot split the air. The clown jerked, fingers loosening, and vanished once more as Sam dropped hard, sucking down the searing night air like cold water.

"You still all right?" Nate asked, lowering his gun and extending his hand again. Sam took it this time.

"Pissed," he rasped, "but I'll live."

The two men surveyed the scene, tense, expectant, weapons ready. A minute passed, another, without an attack or reappearance. Slowly, the crickets resumed their chorus.

"Nate," Sam said hoarsely, "what was that?"

Nate knew what Martin Browne would've called it. His grandfather had been a by-the-Book Baptist preacher, and the topic he'd pounded the hardest had been the demons that supposedly roamed the earth in numbers to rival the angels, who had to be guarded against at every turn because you never knew when or where they were going to show up. But though

Grandpa had often reminded his flock these unholy entities could assume various and sundry guises to carry out their dark works, Nate had a feeling this creature would've thrown even him.

No preacher he, he gave the only answer he could. "I . . . Jesus, Sam, I don't know." His searching gaze caught on something, jerked downward. "What's that?"

"My answer hasn't changed in the two seconds since I asked you."

"No, there." Nate pointed to the ground at Sam's feet. The grass there glistened darkly, wetly, in the moonlight. Nate knelt, touched two fingers to it. They came away red. "Blood," he said, stunned, eyes flicking up to Sam. "I hit it."

"You hurt it." Sam's mind spun. "So no matter what this thing is, we can damage it." He scanned their surroundings, the serrated wall of the woods, black trees whispering to their right and the empty dirt road to their left. "If we can find it again, anyway."

"Or if it finds us."

"Christ, I thought you were supposed to be the optimist."

In reply Nate spit, "There."

Sam spun. The clown was back, between the trees, visible for a teasing instant before turning and disappearing deeper into the woods. They took off after it, snaking through the trees with nerves strung tight and fingers ready to slip around their triggers. They'd been in these woods before, daytime and night. In-season they hunted there. They were as comfortable there as they were in the cruiser, the station, their own homes.

But tonight every patch of ground, no matter how many times they'd trod it beneath their boots, seemed suspect, hostile, as if it might at any moment dart out from under them, trip them up, bump or bulge unexpectedly and send them stumbling straight into their opponent's arms. The woods dripped malevolence, invaded by the malice in the unearthly clown's actions, if missing from its blank painted face. The men heard their heartbeats as cracks of thunder; Sam listened past his, ears keen for any hint of that strange static, those gurgling, glottal voices crawling over each other like blind worms wriggling in a clump of thick black mud.

And silently, and suddenly, the clown appeared and disappeared, a grin in the dark, a specter in oversized shoes. To the left of the men, to the right, ahead, behind. It popped up between them, dappled by the shadows of the trees, and guns barked. Sam's shot clipped the clown's shoulder, another red blossom of blood bursting on the yellow suit, but it vanished before Nate's struck home, the bullet burying itself in a nearby tree.

"We can't keep doing this," Sam said, ears ringing in the silence afterward. "Popping off every time it shows up— we're good shots, but if it keeps pulling this crap we're gonna shoot each other, sooner rather than later. Not to mention we'll probably run out of ammo before this damn thing gets tired of playing with us."

"One of us draws it out, the other shoots," Nate said. "Only thing we can do."

Sam nodded. "All right. Which one of us is bait?"

"Me. You're the best shot on the force."

Sam snorted. "Of course you admit it when there's nobody around to hear."

"Tell you one thing, though." Nate braced himself, readjusting his sweat-slickened grip on his gun.

"Yeah?"

"Next time a circus comes through, my family's not going anywhere near it, I don't care how much they beg me."

"Amen," Sam said, and disappeared into the trees.

Nate moved forward, alone but not alone. Though no shots had proven fatal so far, blood splattered the night-black leaves and streaked the bracken-strewn path, giving him a trail to follow—*and maybe that's exactly what this bastard wants*, an inner voice whispered. He swallowed hard, dry-mouthed, but kept going, every sense alert and his weapon at the ready.

Assuming you get a chance to use it, the same voice pointed out.

Shut up, he snapped back.

And then he saw it, in a small clearing up ahead: the clown, spotlit in bone-colored light from the sickle-shaped moon above. Taking a deep breath, the sense of unreality tugging at him like his shadow, Nate stepped out into the clearing, the twin voids of the clown's eyes locking onto him. An odd hum slithered through his ears, crawled between the bones of his spine. Beads of sweat rolled down his brow to drip from the tip of his nose.

"What's with the disappearing act, huh?" His hoarse challenge rang through the trees. He caught a flicker of movement among them: Sam, getting into position. *Or maybe this thing has a buddy, too.* He shuddered at the thought. "We made you bleed. Seems to me maybe you're afraid to face us like a m—"

The blow came suddenly, the clown's fist driving into Nate's stomach before he realized it'd moved. It struck like a sledgehammer, forcing every bit of breath from his body. As he doubled over, the clown struck again and he dropped, sunbursts of pain exploding behind his eyelids. Leaves rasped against his cheek. Dirt clung to his tongue when he tried to draw a breath.

The clown rolled him over. He drove both feet up, felt his boots sink in as they connected with the thing's stomach, and grunted in satisfaction as it wheeled backwards, bloody

suit rippling like a sail in the wind. He stood, head spinning, and smashed his fist against the clown's face. His knuckles left streaks of blood across its left cheek, but Nate noted distantly no greasepaint came away on his skin.

"*Sam!*" he roared, holding back the clown as its hooked fingers swiped for his face. "*Any time you're ready!*"

The next moment was eternal, and in its ages the thought struck Nate that Sam might already be dead, that this thing might've gotten him while they were separated and then popped into the clearing to take care of him, too, *oh God, Sam*—

The shot came just as Nate broke away, blowing out the back of the thing's skull. He stumbled back as red rain misted his face, spitting to clear the sour copper tang from his lips. At his feet, the clown lay crumpled. He shoved it with his foot and its limbs flopped like oversized fish, but there was no life in the movement. Its eyes stared up, blank as ever, at the night sky, hollow pools of moonlight.

There was a rustle in the brush and Nate jumped, but it was just Sam emerging, holstering his gun. "What'd you do, get lost?" Nate asked, breath slowly normalizing, voice still hoarse.

"You're welcome," Sam said. "Next time I'll blow your head off, too, okay?"

A laugh bubbled up beneath Nate's lips, broke loose. Another followed, and another, and then both men were laughing, knees weak, holding each other up. Sam knew how nuts the scene would seem to anyone who walked in now, and he laughed harder—it was that or scream.

As their hysterical laughter slowly trailed off, the two men straightened, looking down at the bizarre corpse before them. "How the hell do we write this one up?" Nate asked.

"No idea," Sam said, hand on Nate's shoulder, "but I'm so glad it's your turn."

Nate started. "No, it's not. I wrote up that domestic last week, remember? The Larchburgs."

"Yeah, but I wrote up Chris Mitchell's drunk-and-disorderly Monday." It was amazing, Sam thought, how the mind adjusted to something that'd been about to tear it apart. Moments ago they'd been battling an unearthly clown. Now they

were bantering over who'd write it up like they would any routine call. 10-48. Responded 11:02 PM. Clown in the woods. Suspect killed at the scene. Nothin' to see here, folks.

Oh, boy, accounting for these bullets is gonna be fun.

Nate sighed. "Well, at least we've got the body. Maybe the guys at the lab will be able t—"

He cut off. The body was rippling, shifting, beneath its clothes—something was, anyway. As they watched, the clown performed its final trick, melting away into maggots, clumps and clots of the squirming things. Breaking up, they burrowed through gloves, suit, shoes, audibly crawling over each other, fat bodies white as greasepaint. Nate and Sam recoiled, gagging, from the sight, the stench of putrefaction that burst from the frenzied parasites, disbelief warring with disgust.

Nothing remained when the last one disappeared into the dirt, not a scrap of fabric or streak of paint, and for a minute silence reigned over the men as they looked down at the patch of earth where the body had been.

Sam broke it. "Shit," he said, speaking for them both. He looked at Nate. "What now?"

Nate squared his shoulders. "We do our jobs," he said, voice weary but firm. "That's all."

Sam snorted. "Sure. Just do me a favor, will ya? Next time I start complaining a shift's too boring, hit me."

"Gladly." Nate clapped Sam tiredly on the back. "Now c'mon. Let's get going."

But Sam made no move to follow. "Hey, you hear that?"

Nate paused, cocked his head, listened. "No, nothing."

Sam nodded. "Exactly. Still no crickets."

No, there weren't, and a frisson of unease ran up Nate's spine. They'd only fallen silent tonight when . . .

"Probably scared off," he said, pushing the other possibility down deep. "Can't really blame 'em. Give 'em some time. They'll be back."

"Sure. 'Course they will." But Sam couldn't keep from scanning the clearing one more time before shaking himself out. "All right, let's get the hell outta here, huh?"

"Amen, brother."

"What time is it?" Sam asked as they plunged back into the brush.

Nate glanced at his watch. "It's—Christ, past midnight." Sam cursed. "Why? Tania?"

"Yeah," Sam sighed, rubbing his head. "I said I'd be by around—oh, shut *up*," he growled, glaring, catching Nate's chuckle and the grin that flickered across his face in the dark.

"What? I just think it's nice to see you so domestically-minded after all these years."

"Swear to God, Browne, if you don't shut your fucking mouth . . ."

Their voices filling the stillness of the night air, the men made their way back to the car.

©

Story: Sarah Cannavo
Art: Michael Neno

Sarah Cannavo is a writer of prose and poetry haunting southern New Jersey. Her poems and short stories have appeared in anthologies and magazines such as Liminality, Star*Line, Pulp Modern, DBND Publishing's Halloween Horror Volume 3, and JOURN-E, and are forthcoming in Dreams and Nightmares and From the Yonder Volume 3. Her poems "Fallen But Not Down" and "Learning the Way" were nominated for a 2020 and 2021 Rhysling Award, respectively, and her poem "There Goes the Security Deposit" has been nominated for the 2022 Dwarf Stars Awards. Her story "Unreality" and novella Wolf of the Pines are available now on Amazon. Her website is moodilymusing. blogspot.com.

He was sitting straight in bed, covered in sweat, howling.
He saw me and pointed at the window.

Apples in the Attic

M.E. Proctor

In most houses, the attic is hidden behind a trap door with a folding ladder attached to it, unless you live in a grand residence with a real staircase at the end of a hallway, or in one of these artist studios, pictured in movies, clad in glass panes with an unaffordable view of the Paris rooftops, if that can even be called an attic. My grandmother's place was neither of those. Yet, the set-up was unusual. In her house, the attic staircase was hidden in a closet.

I don't remember when I found out. I must have been told because I was a curious kid and never stopped asking questions. Of course, I would ask what was behind that door in my bedroom that I couldn't open. Now that I'm no longer a nosy six-year-old I understand why Grandma locked the closet. She didn't want to have to pick me off the floor with a broken skull after I tumbled down a narrow ladder. After all these years, I still remember her warnings. *Be careful, girl, it's awfully steep.* What's remarkable is that from the moment I was told about the attic, the door was no longer locked and Grandma never forbid me to go up there. She had a keen understanding of reverse psychology. There's little attraction when there's no mystery. She went one step further. She often sent me to the attic to collect the apples she stored up there.

The smell still tickles my nose.

The attic wasn't a scary place. Sunlight slipped through cracks between the roof tiles, glowed around the smudged skylights, lit up the dust motes, and caught the curve of the red and yellow apples lined up like soldiers on parade on the rough splintered boards. Lying in bed at night, I often thought of sleeping in that big space above my head. I would gather

blankets, sheets, and pillows and make a comfortable nest among the fruit and maybe catch that moment when the apples went from glossy to wrinkled without losing the goodness inside. It was the kind of miracle I wanted to witness.

Grandma's cellar was another place of wonder. One small room was black from the coal that used to be stored there. The coal chute was closed by a cast iron grate held in place by a heavy rusty chain, something out of a medieval castle. Another room was fitted with a work bench and contained a variety of tools: hammers, a pickaxe, long screwdrivers, nicked and rusty. I kept away from them. You could get tetanus from these things. A pantry with shelves loaded with preserves, pots and pans occupied one corner, and a large laundry room with vats, buckets and basins that weren't used anymore now that Grandma had a modern washing machine completed the floor plan. The place smelled of soap and starch. I didn't mind going down to the cellar to fetch supplies, but I kept a wary eye for the big hairy spiders that slipped in from the yard. Grandma had told me they often came in pairs. When I spotted one, I called her and she captured it to return it to the yard. To reunite the couple, she said. You didn't want to smash them anyway, they made a worse mess dead than alive.

One of my grandmother's rituals connected the attic and the cellar like a straight life line.

On Fridays, no matter what the weather forecast said, Grandma washed the bedsheets. She'd done it that way like clockwork for fifty years. After dusting the twig of blessed boxwood that garnished the back of the recess by the front door, Grandma had a quiet word with the plaster Virgin Mary enthroned there. She gave the statuette a little nod every time she went by it. I was sure they had an understanding. It explained why most Fridays were dry.

When the Holy Mother collaborated and the day was sunny, we hauled the heavy baskets from the cellar to the yard and hung the sheets to dry. The scent of sundried bedsheets, like the smell of drying apples, sticks in my memory forever. On the rare occasions when rain threatened, we took the load to the attic. Lines were strung, and we tiptoed like ballet dancers, pins in hand, between the apples. It was warm up there, stifling, the air baked with the accumulated heat of summer. The blank canvasses of the white sheets turned the attic into a blinding maze. I remember running up the ladder four, five times a day to check if the laundry was dry. I slipped between the still curtains, picturing what might wait for me behind the next row and the next one after that.

There was never anything, of course, just the apples.

I always spent the summer months at Grandma's. School was out and Mom and Dad were working. I had to go somewhere. One year, I went to camp for a week at the seaside. I didn't care for it much. The realization that sending me to camp was a cost we could barely afford didn't come to me until much later. When told I wouldn't go to camp anymore, I welcomed the news that I would stay at Grandma's for the entire vacation period. Open fields instead of hard sidewalks, a bicycle that I could ride into the wilderness from sunrise to sundown, and a gaggle of friends to run around with. Town wasn't far, but it was a very different world.

There was no attic in my parents' apartment building.

No cellar that I knew of either.

It wasn't a real house. Not like my grandmother's.

When I touched the walls of our apartment in town, I felt nothing. I could put my ear to the wall and hear the neighbors argue. I could hear the water in the pipes when the woman upstairs took a shower or flushed the toilet. But I couldn't feel the house, like I did at Grandma's, where the walls hummed to me and lulled me to sleep. All I heard at the apartment were the people that lived there and would move out one day, replaced by others just like them. My family too would leave. I doubted we'd go live in a house like Grandma's.

There could not be two

houses like hers on the entire planet.

I must have known for a long time, without really *knowing*, that something between these walls was different. I might even have understood some of it over time but it remained vague. There were signs, I just wasn't equipped to interpret them.

One event comes to mind. I must have been nine or ten. My brother Tommy was five years old, no longer a baby or Grandma wouldn't have agreed to take care of him for the summer. I wasn't much of a burden by then. I set off in the morning with a lunch box, and she didn't see me again until sunset. We were a dozen neighborhood kids, always hanging together, safety in numbers. There were occasional sprains and scrapes, fixed with iodine and band aids, sunburns, sometimes cruel, and torn jeans. This was before Neighborhood Watch but the entire neighborhood watched. In exchange for this remarkable degree of freedom, I didn't mind helping with chores around the house and the yard. There were chickens to feed, plants to water, gro-

ceries to pick up.

I had mixed feelings about Tommy joining me at Grandma's. I was concerned he might be a burden and keep me at the house and away from my friends. Mom and Dad wouldn't have responded well to my griping, so I kept my mouth shut. I knew I would have to make the best of it. I packed my bag, watched Mom gather Tommy's things, including his favorite toys, and we set off for Grandma's. She had made lunch. I don't remember what it was but it must have been good because she was a great cook. We had coffee and pie later in the afternoon, then Mom and Dad kissed us goodbye, said they'd be back next weekend, and left. I played a board game with Tommy. We had fun. Everything was fine. We went to bed.

I was in that beginning of sleep, when you don't know if you're dreaming or not. Tommy's scream must have been loud enough to wake the entire street. His room was next door and I got to him before Grandma. He was sitting straight in bed, covered in sweat, howling. He saw me and pointed at the window. It was open with the screen in, and the curtains half drawn. The night was cool and pleasant. There was nothing there, not even the shadow of a tree branch or anything scary like that.

"What's going on?" Grandma said.

Tommy had stopped screaming. He was crying with his face in the pillow.

"I don't know. I think he saw something in the window."

Grandma sat on the side of the bed and reached for Tommy. She touched his shoulder and it was like electricity went through him. He screamed again. Grandma recoiled and stood up. She stuck her hands under her armpits, like she didn't want them to fly out.

"See what's wrong with him, Suzy," she said.

I was afraid he would not let me touch him either, but he wrapped his arms around my waist and put his head in my lap. He was rolled in a ball.

"Home," he muttered. "I want to go home."

"He's homesick," Grandma said. "I'll go make some cocoa. He'll sleep and it will all be all right tomorrow."

Tommy's head popped up. "No!" he yelled. "Home. I want to go home!" His voice was so shrill it broke.

"It's the first time he doesn't sleep at home, I gather," Grandma said.

"We went to aunt Clara's with Mom and Dad for Easter and he was fine," I said.

The look on her face scared me. "What are you saying, girl?"

It was like a hand pressed against my neck and I couldn't swallow. Tommy weighed heavily on my stomach. He was shivering. "He must have had a nightmare," I said.

"Does he have nightmares?"

I couldn't recall Tommy ever having any, but he wasn't in his bed, in his room. Things were different. It must have thrown him. He was so scared his fear was getting to me now. I had to look at the window, I couldn't help it. Maybe there was a shadow, something moving out there, it was hard to say.

"I'll stay with you, Tommy," I said.

The sobbing continued. He muttered, "no, no, home."

"I'll go call your father,"

Grandma said. "Stupid child."

I'd never seen her like that. She could be rough sometimes when she was irritated, but she was never mean. She sounded mean.

"Dad will come?" Tommy whispered through the tears.

"Yes. What was it Tom, what did you see? You had a bad dream?"

He shook his head. "I saw . . . something. At the window. Eyes, oh . . . snake . . ."

"I'll close the window," I said.

He grabbed me so hard it hurt. "It's inside."

His eyes were wild. I'd never seen anybody so terrified.

Grandma appeared in the doorway. "Your father is coming," she said. "Let's get you dressed, boy."

Tommy whispered. "Not her, tell her . . . to go away."

How could I tell my grandmother she wasn't wanted in the room? I looked at her and at that moment she wasn't Grandma anymore. She was a dark stranger and she scared me too.

"Clean him up," she said. "He peed in his pajamas." She went down the stairs. Her steps sounded loud and heavy on the treads.

I led Tommy to the bathroom and helped him. It was warm in there and he was shaking. His arms were covered in goosebumps. When we were done, I took him to my room to wait for Dad. I always slept with the curtains open because I liked to get up in the middle of the night to look at the stars, but I closed the curtains for Tommy. I saw him look at the attic door with that same wild look in his eyes. I didn't tell him what was behind the door. I was sure it would get him howling again.

The doorbell rang and I heard Dad's voice. Tommy was off my bed and down the stairs so fast he was a blur.

I went down and saw that Tommy was wrapped around Dad's legs. Dad asked me if I wanted to come home too. I told him I'd rather stay. I was thinking of my friends and the tree house we were planning to build this summer. I'd have time to work on that if Tommy wasn't in the way. I shook the thought away. It was vile.

"Maybe he's a little young for a sleepover," Dad said. "Next year, maybe."

But Tommy never stayed at

Grandma's. I'm not sure he ever went back upstairs either.

I didn't think much of the incident at the time. It was my brother's first night away from Mom and Dad and he freaked out. Maybe he thought they'd abandoned him. Grandma's weird reaction faded from my memory. I stayed at her place many times after that. Then Dad was promoted at work and we started traveling more, road trips mostly. Grandma came with us on some of these. When her health started failing and she had a stroke, she lived with us for a while until she was well enough to go back home. She died a few years later.

She left the house to me.

The gift was welcome. I was hopping from one drab flat to another, paying off a second-hand car, stretching my history teacher salary so thin it qualified as optic fiber.

It had been a while since I'd been in the house. It was a mess, and nothing like I remembered from these golden summers twenty years ago. Did I really pee in that cobwebby outhouse, did I really wash in that kitchen sink?

My dad was upbeat. Good walls, solid roof, no leaks. "It'll need some work," he said. "I don't trust the electrical wiring." He shook his head. "I can potter around a lot in a house, but I won't touch electricity, Suzy."

"Grandma lived here a long time, Dad. It didn't go up in flames. I think we have a little time to fix stuff. I won't plug in my microwave."

He was surprised I considered living in the house as it was. I couldn't tell him that a presence jumped at me the moment I walked in. Dad was a very rational man. A to B and all that good stuff. I could tell he was concerned.

"You should not have walked out of your rental until the house was ready."

I hugged him and waved goodbye from the front door.

I couldn't tell him this wasn't about plumbing and plugs, and making sure everything was grounded. This was about the walls and what I felt when I touched them. I couldn't tell him that the house would take care of me. I couldn't explain it to myself.

I spent my first night in the attic, with blankets and

pillows, just like I imagined it so many years ago. The apples were long gone. Their smell was long gone too, absorbed in the rafters. The stains on the floor might be from their juices. I wanted to believe that. I found the hooks that we strung the clotheslines from. Maybe the magic would work if I hung clean bedsheets.

With that half-assed plan in the back of my mind, I went to bed.

I slept soundly. I always slept soundly in Grandma's house.

It wasn't Friday. I couldn't do laundry yet.

There were other rituals I could revive, however. I bought a plaster Virgin Mary in a thrift shop. Finding a twig of blessed boxwood was more complicated but a doddering parish priest helped me. He wanted to confess me and I batted away his entreaties. I didn't know what I was after but it sure wasn't salvation. My next stop was city hall and the library. Digging in property records and old news articles. I took my stack of notes to the attic. The picture was coming together. My great grandfather bought

the land when a farmer died without heirs and his property was divided in lots. Compared to other buyers, my ancestor got an advantageous deal. Something about an underground spring that made the terrain unstable. It didn't seem to hinder construction. The house went up. It was paid off remarkably fast, considering this was the Great Depression. Through world wars and economic crises the house and my forebears thrived, in their modest, inconspicuous bubble.

I reread my notes by the light of a Coleman lantern. I descended from lucky people. Not the kind that won the lottery, but the kind that found favorable currents, like birds that angled their wings just right.

Was there anything wrong with that?

I wanted to believe there wasn't. My ancestors didn't enrich themselves. My parents lived off a government pension. I inherited a house that most people my age would deem unsuitable. If there was a pact with the Devil, the horned one was a third-rate demon specializing in low mortgage interest rates.

I laughed.

Nothing struck me dead.

Friday, it rained and I did laundry. I wished I had a crate of apples to line up in the attic. I hummed a song Grandma sang when she hung the sheets. I knew what it was, I used an app to figure it out. *Fascination*. Nat King Cole had a great version.

The sheets looked good. Big white slabs slicing the span of the attic. The light from the skylights drew enticing shadows on them. I sat on my improvised bed, in my pillow nest, and waited. I hoped I had done everything right. After twenty years, the details were a bit sketchy.

When the sun went down, I thought I smelled apples.

I didn't move. I inhaled the memories.

The show started. On the white canvas in front of me. A man dressed in black, with a bowler hat, and handlebar mustaches lifted a heavy hammer with a long handle high in the air. It came down without a sound. A shadow crumpled at his feet. The image leached from the sheet. Another man walked on the stage of the shadow theater.

He wore a soldier's uniform and carried a pickaxe. He swiped sideways and a shape rolled out of the frame of the bedsheet. This man didn't vanish like the other one. He stood in front of a woman now. He pushed her down. I knew what he was doing. The rendering was crude but there was no room for doubt. He was raping her. This scene didn't end swiftly like the others. It repeated, and repeated. I was about to scream for them to stop when the stage changed. A crib. The woman reached to take the baby. Then there was the man and the woman again. They struggled. She had a pointy tool in her hand. She struck him.

The canvas went blank. The light in the attic was gone. This had all happened in silence, but the silence was deeper now. The strain of watching the shadows made me sleepy.

I woke up late. The sun was striping the attic and the sheets. They were dry. I took them down and folded them. They had no story to tell me anymore.

Three murders that nobody knew about, except me and this house. Great grandfather, grandfather and Grandma. I went to stand against the wall.

I put my hands flat against the brick.

"I hope you don't expect to be fed or anything of the kind," I said. "Because I love you. I slept the best nights of my life under your roof. I dreamed the sweetest dreams. The stars from my bedroom window were the brightest I've ever seen. There is no violence in me but I swear I will destroy you brick by brick, beam by beam, if you ever whisper an evil thought in my ear."

There was a light wave under my palms, and a surge of heat.

"I know what you did to Tommy."

It wasn't a wave now, more a vibration.

"I had a bad thought. I regret it. It was selfish. Because Tommy might have kept me from my friends for a few hours. You scared him, you made him cry, and you awoke the darkness in Grandma. I forgive you because you believed you were doing right by me." I slapped the wall real hard. "No more. You don't read my mind. This stops now."

The vibration subsided.

I hoped we were in a-greement, but I would be on guard.

And the old electrical wiring had to go. Dad was right, the place was a fire hazard.

©
Story: M.E. Proctor
Art: Michael Neno

M.E. Proctor is currently working on a series of contemporary detective novels. The first book in the series will come from TouchPoint Press in January 2023. Her short stories have been published in *Mystery Tribune*, *Shotgun Honey*, *Pulp Modern Flash*, *Bristol Noir*, *Fiction on the Web*, *The Bookends Review* and others. She lives in Livingston, Texas. On Twitter: @MEProctor3.

CIRSOVA® *Presents*

Cirsova Publishing is closing 2022 with a bang, bringing you the finest in high-octane thrilling action and adventure!

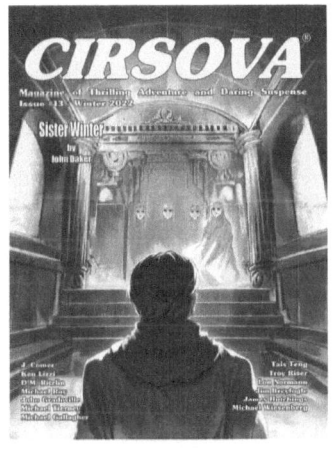

Michael Tierney's Orphan of the Shadowy Moon concludes in Winter along with Dave Ritzlin's Vran, the Chaos-Warped! Plus the final arc of Jim Breyfogle's Mongoose and Meerkat is underway! New original exciting fiction from fan favorites and fresh faces alike!

Cirsova Magazine V2. #13 is Out December 15th, 2022!

Plus, out now is the fully illustrated edition of Michael Tierney's Wild Stars V: The Artomique Paradigm.

Expanded with bonus content, including some of the earliest Wild Stars short stories and new original art by DarkFilly, this is a Sword & Planet romp you won't want to miss!

Available through Amazon.com!

All of this and more from Cirsova Publishing!

http://www.cirsova.wordpress.com

It was too late to do anything, though. The girl was gone, disappeared into thin air, and I didn't know how to call her back or if it was even possible.

You Were the Last

Brandon Barrows

Some years ago, after I left my father's organization and before I owned *Kagutsuchi-jyuu*, the divine firearm I've come to rely on so much lately, I was on a lonely road in Nagano, heading back to Tokyo after a visit with the priest of the main shrine in the town where I was raised. It was past midnight and the height of the rainy season. A storm raged all around me, but the road was smooth and well-maintained. I had a feeling of floating, as if I was suspended in mid-air, the rain rushing past me rather than the opposite.

I knew a great deal about the Other Shore even then, but not as much about the natural world as I would have liked. I was at a crossroads. Reverend Kataoka was the closest thing I had to a friend just then and the talk helped, but my thoughts were still unsettled and I was half-lost in them, not paying as much attention as I should have been, when I noticed frantic motion on the shoulder of the road. I slowed the car and pulled off the pavement. The headlights picked out a woman, her face starkly white in their glare, waving her arms at me.

I was on alert and for the moment, my troubles disappeared. The road clung to the side of a steep hill, with just enough shoulder for a breakdown lane. On the opposite side, past a barrier, the road fell away towards a shallow valley. There was nothing around for some distance in either direction and I saw no other vehicle anywhere. Where had this woman come from?

I rolled down the window and she hurried towards me.

Closer up, I could see that she was young, not much beyond twenty. Her hair was long and hung in tangles that clung to her shoulders and her fine, white throat. She wore a light-colored blouse, so thin it was see-through with the water soaking it, and a skirt that fell to just past her knees. I saw no shoes, but she had feet, at least. That made up my mind.

"Get in," I told her, unlocking the passenger door. She came around quickly, threw open the door, and slipped inside.

I turned the heat up, figuring the girl must be freezing. I caught a whiff of something unpleasant, like mold or mildew—the kind that accumulates in the corners of old cellars. I made no mention of it; it must have been the girl and I didn't want to embarrass her. Instead I asked, "Are you okay? Where did you come from?"

In answer, she gripped the sleeve of my jacket. "Please!" It was barely a whisper. "You have to help me." Her eyes were large and caught the faint light from the dashboard and headlights. In them, I saw desperation, fear, and something I couldn't quite identify.

"I will. Relax."

"You don't understand!" she said, louder now, her grip tighter. "You have to go, right now. He's going to kill me!"

Wariness surged. "Who?"

"My husband." She looked directly into my eyes and something electric leapt up my spine. "He's going to kill me," she said again.

No matter what was going on, there was no point sitting on the side of the road and I wasn't so cruel I'd toss the girl back outside. I put the car in motion. "You had a fight with your husband, huh?"

"I tried to leave him. He said he's going to kill me for it."

I wanted to reassure her, to comfort her and say something like "Oh, he can't really mean that," but I had met plenty of men who would say it and mean it. He could be one of them. I just didn't know.

"There's a town not too far from here, in the direction I'm heading. We'll find the local police and they'll take care of you."

The girl didn't respond, but I could hear her softly crying.

"What's your name?"

"Sawako . . . Yoneda."

"I'm Azuma Kuromori," I told her, but she didn't seem to care one way or the other, so I kept quiet, concentrating on driving through the storm and the night.

The town appeared suddenly from behind a bend in the hills. We were in the middle of nowhere and then we were on the outskirts of the town. Sporadically spaced houses lined the road, interspersed with flooded fields. The road became narrower and streetlights more frequent.

I had no phone-service, so my only option was to look for some business that might be open, some place that could direct me to the police. I saw a gas-station and a convenience-store, both national chains I expected to have twenty-four-hour service, but neither were open. I supposed the town was too small to warrant operating around the clock. After fifteen minutes of crawling the streets, I asked if the girl knew the town, but she didn't answer. Even her crying stopped and she merely stared ahead, her face blank. A cold feeling went through me despite the heater.

Eventually, on the far side of town, I found a *minshuku*, the kind of scaled-down lodgings that would be called a bed and breakfast in the west. There was a sign out front, but no lights were on, either outside or in. The dashboard clock said it was nearly two a.m., but I had to take a chance. I couldn't keep driving around all night with this girl.

I parked, cut the engine, then hopped out, opened the girl's side and practically dragged her out. "C'mon. Let's see if they can help us." I thought she nodded, but couldn't be sure.

Under the roof of a shallow porch, I knocked on the front door. There was no response at first, but I kept it up and a light went on inside. The door opened. A late-middle-aged man peered out at me. His face was narrow, the skin stretched tightly across sharp cheekbones, with deep lines on either side of a small mouth. His eyes looked kind, but there was caution in them, too.

"What do you want? It's so late," he complained.

"I'm very sorry," I told him, bowing from the shoulders. "I

wouldn't bother you except I found this girl alongside the road a ways back. She says her husband wants to kill her. I need to speak with the police and I don't know this town at all."

Something I might have called fear appeared on the innkeeper's face, then disappeared, replaced by a look so bland and benign he might have been a monk on the verge of enlightenment. "What girl?" he asked.

I turned and found that I was alone. "What the—? Where did she go?"

He shook his head. "I saw only you, sir. You must be very tired. Been driving long?" He showed me a weary smile, as if tolerance was an indulgence he was willing to offer me.

I looked in every direction. It was only seconds since I saw her; if she left, even if she were running, I should still be able to see her. I didn't. I went back to the car, thinking she returned to it, but it was empty.

Soaked to the bone now and with no other options, I got my overnight bag from the trunk and went back to the *minshuku*. The owner still stood under the cover of the porch. "Do you want a room, sir?"

"Yes," I told him. "And a phone."

I was in a *kimono* and sipping hot tea, both provided by Mrs. Wada, the innkeeper's wife, when there was a knock on the door of my room. Mrs. Wada was not as gracious or accommodating as her husband, but she was glad to take the fistful of bills I offered for my lodging. Now, as the door slid open, she seemed disapproving again as she announced that Officer Saito had arrived to see me.

The officer thanked her, entered, and shut the door behind himself. He turned, bowed to me, and introduced himself. I bowed back and did the same.

"I'm sorry to get you out of bed, especially on a night like this," I told the other man. He was older than me, and probably had experience in his work, but even in uniform, he gave off the air of a displaced farmer. In this area, he might well have been.

"It's no problem," he assured me. "When I got your

call, I was eager to speak with you, truth be told."

I would hope so. I would think the report of a missing girl, claiming her husband wanted to kill her, should interest any law-enforcement officer. In the life I'd recently left, contacting the police was something I would have avoided at all costs. I didn't yet know what I wanted to do going forward, but this seemed like a good place to start breaking old habits.

Still, I didn't want to get dragged into this matter anymore than I already was.

"I told you everything there is to tell when I called you," I told Saito. "I don't mean to be rude, but shouldn't you be looking for her? Every moment we sit here is another she has to wander around out there. And if what she said about her husband is true, he might be looking for her, too. Shouldn't you—"

"Please forgive me, Kuromori-san," the cop interrupted. "There is more to this than you know and if you are the man I believe you are, I would ask that you listen to what I have to say."

Something flickered in the back of my brain. Saito might have looked like a hick, but I suspected it was cultivated. He didn't speak like just any rural community patrol officer.

I offered Saito tea and when he accepted, we sat on the *tatami*. He sipped and said, "Very good. I haven't had Mrs. Wada's tea in some time. May I begin my story?"

"Sure," I told him.

"About a year ago, I got a call from this very inn. There was a scuffle between a guest and a local. The guest was a salesman of some sort, just passing through, and outside of town, he picked up a hitchhiking girl. She told him she was leaving her abusive husband. He already made a reservation here, so he brought her along and asked for a second room, explaining to the Wadas that there was nothing untoward between them, she was just a girl he wanted to help, at least for the night. The Wadas are good people and they understood. Along about ten o'clock, however, the girl's husband showed up. One way or the other, he discovered her whereabouts and decided he was going to drag her home.

The Wadas are older and not fighters, but this salesman tried to stand up for the girl. I was called, but by the time I got here, the girl had fled and her husband set out after her."

"So she's done this before?" I asked.

Saito held up a hand and continued as if I hadn't spoken. "They had the girl's name and I knew where she and her husband lived. It's a cabbage farm off the main highway, some distance from town. I went out there and found only the husband, who admitted he was at the inn, but said that the girl ran out while he was fighting with the salesman and he never found her. He allowed me to search his home, but I found nothing out of the ordinary and no girl.

"When I returned here, the salesman told me his story but declined to press any charges. He was afraid of it getting back to his employer and his family. I believe he really didn't mean anything inappropriate towards the girl, but I understood why he would want to keep the situation quiet. He paid the Wadas for some damage done to the rooms and left right away, too embarrassed to even stay the rest of the night.

"I searched for the girl all night and in the morning, called in help from the neighboring towns, but we never found her. Her husband swore he had not found her, either, and we couldn't prove otherwise. As you've probably already guessed, the girl's name was Sawako Yoneda. Her husband's name is Suguru, and even before this incident, he had a reputation as a brutal man. I was certain that he did something to the girl, but there was no evidence to support the idea."

"Am I correct in guessing the girl was never seen again? Until tonight, I mean."

Saito shook his head. "No, actually." He sipped tea, emptying his cup, then said, "Several months ago, right at the height of winter, a man just passing through called me with a story much the same as yours. He picked up a woman who said her name was Sawako Yoneda. She was walking along the side of the road wearing clothing too thin for the weather and without any shoes. She told him her husband was going to kill her and she needed help. He stopped at the gas station to use the phone, cellphone service being spotty out here, and after he made the call, he turned to find she was gone."

"Strange."

"Yes, to put it mildly. But tell me what you think of this. Just a few weeks ago, I got a call, again from this inn. An older couple visiting relatives stayed the night here and on their way out of town, picked up a girl along the highway, who gave her name as Sawako and said she was trying to escape her husband. They turned around, came back here, and while the gentleman came inside to make the call, his wife stayed in their car with the girl. The woman sat up front and the girl in the back. The whole ride into town, the woman asked questions, but the girl's answers only related to how she needed to escape her husband. As the car pulled up to the inn and the husband got out, the wife told Sawako that everything would soon be taken care of and asked if she had anyone she could stay with. There was no answer. She turned around and the girl was gone. The

woman was absolutely certain the back doors had not been opened and that there was no other way for her to get out of the car.

"And now, Kuromori-san, I have you . . . at this same inn, telling me so similar a story. If you are related to the Kuromori-san that I believe you are, perhaps you can tell me what is going on here."

Saito seemed to know who I was, at least who my father was, and that I was that man's son. How he knew, I couldn't guess. My father was a secretive person and his organization was the same. A simple country cop shouldn't even know of its existence, but clearly Saito was more than that.

"Is Sawako-san a ghost, perhaps?" Saito asked. "I was convinced, after the night she first disappeared, that Yoneda-san killed her and secreted her body away, but I could never prove it. I never had anything to go on besides my instinct and, sad to say, that doesn't count for much in a court of law."

I poured more tea into Saito's cup, then refreshed my own. "I don't know what you have here." There was no point pretending I didn't understand what he was talking about and now that I knew a little more, it explained Wada the innkeeper's look of fear, too. "If I hadn't seen this girl for myself, I'd chalk it up to an urban legend, on par with the taxi-driver and the disappearing fare to the graveyard." I sipped from my cup. "I'll tell you one thing, though: I saw that girl's feet."

Saito laughed, though I wasn't making a joke. He set down his tea-cup and stood, bowing slightly. "Thank you for your report on this matter, Kuromori-san, and thank you for listening to my story. I know you must be very tired and would like to get some sleep."

I stood as well. We shook hands.

Saito moved to the door and stopped. "If you would be so kind," he began. "Would you give this matter some thought and, if you think of anything, please call me? I'm sure you're in a hurry to be on your way, but I would very much appreciate any assistance you might provide."

"Sure, if I think of anything,"

I said, noncommittally.

Saito dipped his head, slid the door open, and disappeared.

I lay in bed, eyes closed, but awake despite my tiredness and the softness of the *futon*. My conversation with Saito erased any desire to sleep. I tried to tell myself that whatever was happening wasn't my problem, that I did my duty as someone trying to be a good citizen by reporting everything I knew to the police. Let Saito deal it with it. It was his job after all.

But was it? He seemed accepting of the possibility of the supernatural, and he clearly had some awareness of it if he knew about my father, who made Nagano his home some twenty years earlier. That didn't mean he was capable of dealing with whatever the girl represented, though.

And what of Sawako Yoneda herself? Was she *yurei*? Some *bakemono* simply using the girl's shape? Girl, ghost, or *yokai* though, there was real fear in her eyes. And something else, too, that it took me too long to recognize: an appeal for help too desperate even for her words to convey. Only the eyes, the so-called windows to the soul, could express her true need and I was too blind to see it in the moment.

It was too late to do anything, though. The girl was gone, disappeared into thin air, and I didn't know how to call her back or if it was even possible.

I rolled over, trying to find a more comfortable position and became aware that I was no longer alone.

Slowly, I opened my eyes and she was there. Even in the darkness, I could see her plainly. The fine features, the tangled mass of hair, and the anguish in her eyes. Everything was as I remembered.

"Sawako-san," I whispered, reaching a hand towards the figure.

She was already gone. There was nothing so dramatic as a flash of light or a wavering as she faded away. One second she was there, the next she simply wasn't.

I lay back, shaken, knowing there was no chance of ever sleeping now and no longer even wanting to. I listened to the rain pounding against the roof, the splash of water running from the gutters, and all I could think of was tears in a young girl's eyes and the soft sound of her crying as we drove through the night.

I climbed out of bed, switched on the light, and went out into the foyer to use the phone.

By morning, the rain had lightened into a gray mist. I sat in the passenger seat of Saito's car, an older Toyota Crown. "Yoneda-san only knows about the driver this past winter, not the couple who also saw Sawako-san," he told me in answer to my question.

"What exactly did you tell him?"

Saito glanced at me. "Only that a woman calling herself Sawako Yoneda was seen."

"This time, you'll tell him that someone found Sawako wandering, sick and delirious, and took her to the hospital. The doctors say she's in bad shape, but she's expected to make a full recovery and you plan to question her about where she's been all this time."

Saito shook his head, his eyes never leaving the road. "Yoneda-san won't believe it. I'm sure he killed her last year."

"I don't think so. You said he has a reputation for brutality."

The officer nodded.

"So he wouldn't make it easy on her, is my guess. He would want his wife to suffer as long as possible for the insult of daring to leave him."

Saito looked at me again. "You might be right, but . . . do you really think he's been keeping her somewhere? I searched the place and didn't find anything."

I remembered the look in the girl's eyes. "I really don't think she's dead."

The car slowed for a turn as we left the main road. "I don't know about the legality of this plan of yours, Kuromori-san, but I'm willing to give it a try."

"If it turns out I'm right, I don't think there'll be any blowback and if there is, I'll take responsibility."

"No," Saito said. "The responsibility is mine." The way he said it left no room for argument.

The car pulled to a stop by a dense stand of trees. Saito pointed and said, "The Yoneda property begins maybe three-hundred yards beyond this point. If you go through the woods, you'll see the buildings."

"Okay. Give me ten minutes and then go on up."

Saito nodded. I got out and hurried in the direction he indicated.

Past the trees, the ground sloped gently upwards and I found myself on a rise overlooking the Yoneda farm. Between the hill and the buildings was a wide area of tilled soil, the green heads of cabbages lined up in rows. The rest of the farm consisted of a house, a freestanding garage, and a couple of outbuildings for equipment and storage. I found a good view of the house, then I waited.

Only a minute or two passed before Saito's patrol-car came into view. It crawled up to the house. A man, who seemed large even at a distance, exited the house before Saito even turned the engine off. He met Saito halfway to the car, his body-language making it clear he had no interest in whatever the officer had to say. But Saito spoke to him, anyway. Suguru Yoneda gestured towards the road, then Saito returned to the car, started it, made a tight U-turn and left. Yoneda watched the car until he was sure Saito was really gone and then strode towards the side of the house.

I took that as my cue

and hurried towards the buildings. By the time I made it to the house, Yoneda was just disappearing around the side of the garage. Behind it, shrubs grew thick and wild, clinging to the building and spreading out towards a rise on the opposite side of the property, similar to the one I came down over. Yoneda, even bigger than I guessed from a distance, pushed his way through a narrow path among the brush and stopped at a point two-thirds of the way down the wall of the garage. He stooped, pushed aside a particularly large bush and exposed a metal door, so low it was nearly flush with the ground. He took from his pocket a key ring, selected a key, opened a padlock with it, then pulled up the door and disappeared through it.

As I approached, I heard the meaty sound of flesh on flesh, followed by a high, keening noise like a wounded animal. It hurried my step and I rushed through the brush. No longer caring if Yoneda heard me or what the consequences would be, I practically fell down the stairs into the hidden cellar.

It was dim, the only light coming from a 25-watt bulb hanging from the ceiling, but I could make out the girl, filthy and even thinner than the visions saw, laying on a thin blanket spread across the dirt floor. She had a hand raised, but it did nothing to ward off the blows her husband rained down on her narrow belly.

Rage painted the scene a deep red. Without thinking, I charged forward. The huge man became aware of me and turned, one giant fist swinging upwards and then down, slamming into my shoulder with the force of a sledgehammer. It knocked me off course, but I managed to fall forward, wrapping my arms around the bigger man's waist and dragging us both to the floor.

Yoneda's body was solid as the steel door of this prison and his fists were like stone, pounding against my back over and over again, forcing the breath from my lungs with each blow. I threw short punches into his ribs and kidneys, trying to break his hold on me, trying to get the leverage I needed to make him feel some of the pain he inflicted on his wife.

It was no good; I had some training in combat, but Yoneda's size and strength were more than enough to compensate. More than that, he seemed to be enjoying himself. I caught flashes of his face as we struggled, and each time there was less fury and more joy in his features.

When Yoneda lifted an arm for another blow, I threw myself to the side, trying to escape his grasp. I managed to free one arm, but Yoneda kept hold of me. If anything, he held me tighter, as if he'd given up beating me and decided to simply crush me instead.

My hand crawled blindly over the dirt floor, trying to find something, anything that I could use as a weapon. I wanted to call out to Sawako, telling her to run, to escape, but I had no breath for words and I doubted she could move, anyway.

Something in my chest was about to give. The red of anger faded and the room began to darken. Then my flailing fingers closed around something thin and hard. I gathered every ounce of power left in me and slammed whatever it was into Suguru Yoneda's, feeling the thing compress in my hands as something in the man's face broke. He howled in pain and fury and I swung again, but

missed as he thrashed around.

It didn't matter. Saito's voice said, "Hold it! There's a gun on you both!"

I ignored the warning and brought the thing in my hands down onto Yoneda's face once more, feeling another satisfying crunch.

"Kuromori-san! That's enough!"

I decided Saito was right and rolled onto my side, heaving for breath. A stab of pain told me a rib or two was cracked. I glanced at the thing in my hands; it was a metal water-bowl, like a dog would drink out of, now dented and blood-splattered. I tossed it away in disgust.

I managed to get to one knee. Saito was leaning over Suguru Yoneda, handcuffing him and advising him of his rights. That done, he turned to me. "You might have killed him."

I looked at Sawako Yoneda, cowering on the filthy blanket, her eyes huge and luminous as when I first saw her, but her face so painfully thin I could have wept. "Maybe I should have," I said.

Saito didn't answer.

We sat in the coffee-shop of the closest hospital. After Sawako was admitted, an emergency room doctor taped my ribs. Initial diagnosis was that Sawako was badly abused, but should recover in time. They would know more after a thorough examination. Saito offered to treat me to breakfast as we waited for news. Suguru Yoneda was left in the custody of officers from a nearby town, so there was little for either of us to do.

Neither of us spoke for some time, then he finally broke the silence. "What made you so sure that Sawako-san was alive?"

I sipped coffee and considered. I didn't know exactly, but I felt I should try to answer. "I don't know what I picked up on the road. I don't think it was a ghost, but sometimes, when people are close to death, they're in a sort of between place that's neither here nor the Other Shore, but connected to both. What I saw, when I looked into Sawako-san's eyes, though . . . it was an appeal only the living can make. She was alive and she wanted to keep living, no matter what."

A nurse approached our table. "Officer? The doctor says you may see Mrs. Yoneda for a few minutes. She's in room two-oh-four."

Saito thanked her and she went away. He said to me, "You go, Kuromori-san."

"Me? I don't think—"

"No." Saito was firm. "She'll want to see you. There will be plenty of time for me to ask her about the things I need to know. I'm not going anywhere, after all."

I saw his point.

I found my way to room two-oh-four. The same nurse who informed Saito he could see the girl was waiting outside. She showed surprise at seeing me, instead of the policeman, but only said, "No more than five minutes, please," then opened the door for me.

Sawako Yoneda lay flat on the bed. A network of tubes and machinery were connected to her. She seemed very small and fragile. But her eyes were open and they focused on me.

I stood by the side of the bed, unsure of what to say. "Mrs. Yoneda . . ." I began.

Her hand moved feebly, but it was clear she was trying to reach me. I put my hand on hers. She squeezed my fingers, light as the touch of a feather. Her lips moved. Between her weakness and the oxygen mask covering her mouth, I couldn't hear her. I lowered my ear to her mouth. Barely audible she said, "You were the last." I looked into her eyes. Tears ran down her cheeks. "You were my very last try."

I felt my own eyes begin to sting and burn. Twelve hours earlier, I'd been at a crossroads, directionless and with no idea of the way forward. Now I knew what path I wanted to take.

Gently, I squeezed Sawako's hand back.

Brandon Barrows is the author of several novels for adult audiences in the crime, mystery, and western genres, and the YA fantasy novel *3rd LAW: Mixed Magical Arts*. He has also published more than one-hundred short stories and nearly two-hundred individual comic book issues. He was a Mustang Award finalist in both 2021 and 2022 and a 2022 Derringer Award nominee. Find more at www.brandonbarrowscomics.com and on Twitter @BrandonBarrows

©
Story: Brandon Barrows
Art: Brad Foster

Volume Two

THE COLLECTED ADVENTURES OF
David Cranmer's

TEXAS 67
KR·7195

THE
DRIFTER
DETECTIVE

Garnett Elliott

Alec Cizak

David Cranmer

UNCLE B.
PUBLICATIONS

CRIME FICTION LIVES HERE

*"I'm going to give you something.
You didn't get it from me. Only use it on John Henry Francis.
He's the only one who deserves it."*

Rejection

Stanley Rutgers

Chris Clark

He lounged on the roof of his apartment building, reading the latest issue of *Arbogast Fantasy and Horror*. None of the stories in it had been written by him. The first concerned vampires. It did nothing original but make for its setting a hockey camp in New Jersey. The next involved a serial killer. Following that bit of originality? A five-thousand-word cliché about alien abduction. Chris Clark flipped through the magazine, reading a page or two of each tale. When he got to the finale, a yawner about zombies feeding on a group of fishermen from Boston, he tossed the journal off the roof. It landed in the leaves of a palm tree.

"Good," he said. "Rats will use it to build a nest." He folded up his blue canvas chair and headed back into his apartment building.

As he made his way down the stairs and through the hallway, greeting his neighbors along the way, he scrunched his lips to refrain from shouting. His past tantrums had drawn warnings from management. Upon receiving a rejection notice from *Arbogast Fantasy and Horror*, he usually threw his blue chair around his room, denting the walls.

The slips were always the same. Photocopied, standard memos. "Dear," it read, followed by a blank filled in with his name, handwritten. "We regret to inform you that we cannot use your story at this time." The magazine's editor, John Henry Francis, signed the note with a rubber stamp. He reminded Chris of the guard at the gates of Kafka's "Before

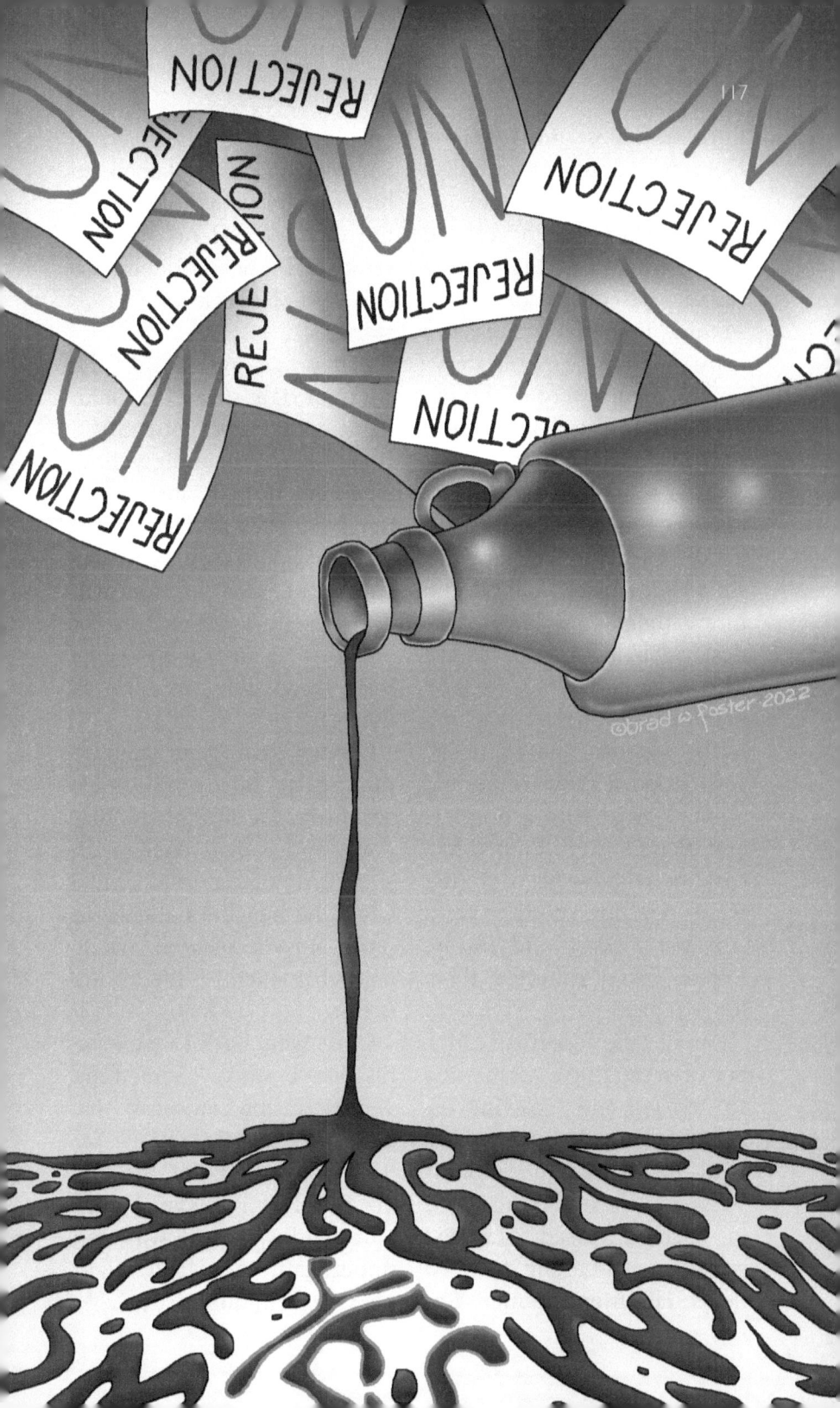

the Law." He assumed, by John Henry's inability to publish anything remotely literary, the douchebag had never read or even heard of Franz Josef Kafka. He once considered sending John Henry Francis a copy of "In the Penal Colony" with a pseudonym in the by-line, certain the editor would be dumb enough to reject it.

Chris slammed the door to his apartment as he stepped inside. He removed his black shirt and black pants and threw them onto his bed. A desk wobbled on loose legs next to the bed, which took up half the space in the bachelor's unit. Against the opposite wall stood a mini-fridge and a small table with a hotplate and blender on it. Pinned to a corkboard above his computer were rejection notices from *Arbogast Fantasy and Horror*. Fifteen. He'd collected them for two years.

Lately, the span of time between sending a submission to *Arbogast* and receiving the rejection form had narrowed. In the beginning, three months passed before he received his self-addressed stamped envelope containing the bad news. His friend Gunter Fry, an older writer who lived in Santa Monica, explained to him exactly what to look for the day John Henry Francis removed his head from his ass and accepted one of Chris's stories.

"They always send the contract right away," he said. "You won't get your SASE back. There'll be a big yellow envelop stuffed into your mailbox. Professional places like *Arbogast*, they send the check out with the contract. They want to take care of business as fast as possible. Snag those rights as soon as they can."

Gunter had been getting published since the mid-seventies. He fought in Vietnam and came back with some gruesome stories. Unlike Chris, he had the patience to write novels as well. Made enough money to live by the ocean.

Chris went back to work on his latest story, "Something Terrible in the Darkness." He had gotten inspiration for it while waiting for the bus at Beverly Boulevard and Normandie. A walkway ran underneath the street, right next to a middle school. At one time, students must have used the tunnel. Chain link gates closed off the entrances on each corner. A quick glance into the dim stairwell leading to the underground revealed walls molested by graffiti. He asked himself, "Just what lurks down there in the pitch? Why aren't children allowed to go there anymore?"

He invented a *new* monster. Not a vampire. Not a werewolf. And for Christ's sake, not a zombie. A creature born from the concrete, from the brutality of the inner city. A beast feeding on anyone foolish enough to look further into those tunnels.

He'd worked on it for two months. He wrote the first draft, let it sit for a few weeks, then set to revising. He called it plumbing. It involved making sure the mechanics of the story made sense. After another draft or two, he hammered the prose into a smooth read. Every writer he knew in Los Angeles complimented him on how tight his prose had gotten. Few of them approved of his subject matter. They were literary snobs. He argued that Kafka authored horror stories.

"At the very worst," they responded, "Kafka might have been dabbling in magical realism."

Chris fine-tuned the seventh draft of "Something Terrible in the Darkness" and printed it. He wrote a standard cover letter detailing his publication credits and a short synopsis of the story, attached a SASE, and stuffed it all into a giant, yellow envelope.

Mailing a story to *Arbogast* had become a ritual. He walked to the Sanford Station post office on Sixth Street and Harvard. A line of people packed the lobby in a half-circle. No more than two employees ever worked at any given moment.

He waited twenty minutes to step up to a window. The clerk behind it, an elderly woman with thin hair, dyed red, identified by a crooked name tag as Roberta, seemed to compete with a snail somewhere, seeing if she could move half as fast. Since Chris didn't have to teach that day, he didn't mind the two minutes it took her to weigh the envelope and put a stamp on it.

Her fingers moved in slow

motion as she typed the weight into her computer and, even slower, turned and said, "Dollar seventy-eight."

Chris paid her, thanked her, and went back home to write a new story.

Five days after mailing "Something Terrible in the Darkness," his SASE sat in his mailbox. His own handwriting grinned at him. "What the hell?" A Korean family got off the elevator the moment he shouted. As they passed him, the father shook his head.

Chris put his hands and the fresh rejection letter in his pockets. He squeezed down on his thighs to remind himself not to get angry in public. Instead of returning to his apartment, he headed for the bus stop at Normandie and Third.

"That sonofabitch," he said. "Five days? Are you kidding me? That piece of shit didn't even read the story!"

He got on the Line 206, headed north to Santa Monica Boulevard where he caught the number 4 express to the west side. Rush hour. Every seat occupied, forcing him to stand, hold on to the bar

overhead while containing his rage. It took ninety minutes to cross town. As soon as he saw the horizon vanish over the ocean and the generic rollercoaster and Ferris wheel on the pier, he relaxed. He got off at Santa Monica's version of Third Street and hustled over to Montana Avenue. Gunter lived down the road from the Aero theater. Chris, in fact, met Gunter at the old cinema. The Aero had been running a series of horror movies. One of them, *The Hollywood Cocaine Massacre*, had been based on a book by Gunter and he'd been invited to speak before the screening. In classic Gunter Fry fashion, he badmouthed the film and Hollywood and showed the audience both his middle fingers before storming out of the building.

Chris had followed him, awestruck by his audacity. "I got to buy you a drink," he said. Gunter being, like most writers, unable to turn down such an offer, agreed. He took him on as an apprentice of sorts, telling him what to read and where to submit his stories.

As he made his way down

the palm tree-lined street, he saw that Gunter's car, a rust brown 1957 Chevy, sat in his small driveway next to his yellow, stucco house. Battling knee-high grass, he trudged across the front lawn and knocked. He waited and beat on the door again, louder.

Gunter Fry ripped it open. A short man, maybe five-two, his dark, wild eyes, marbles, almost, raced up and down and side to side, barely contained behind giant, square glasses. "Chris Clark," he said. "'The hell brings you to Santa Monica?"

"I need to know the secret."

"Kid," he said, "there's no secret. How many times have I told you?"

"You and I know that's bullshit." He moved forward, insisting Gunter let him in. "The hacks are published while the Philip K. Dick's starve."

Gunter stepped aside. "You better not be calling me a hack, kid. I'll crack your larynx with the edge of my hand."

Inside, Chris paced between a glass display case holding Hugo awards Gunter had won and a neon-orange couch fashionable in 1977. "That's just it," he said. "You're one of the only great writers being published today. There *has* to be a secret."

"Ever read any of my work?" Gunter asked.

Chris looked away. "Of course."

Gunter laughed. "I know for a fact that you haven't."

"I read your last book. You don't believe me, go ahead and quiz me."

"But you never read any of the *first* stories I published."

"How do you know?"

"Trust me," he said. "You wouldn't want to."

"I'm sure they're awesome." Chris paced faster. "I have to know what the trick is, how to get past the dragon at the gates."

"Chris," Gunter said, "I'm having dinner with Mary's sister and brother-in-law at six. I've got to get ready."

"Just tell me what I need to do to get that jackass at *Arbogast* to consider my work."

Gunter looked at his watch. "All right," he said. "I'm going to give you something. You didn't get it from me. Only use it on John Henry Francis. He's the only one who deserves it."

The old writer disappeared into his den and returned after a minute with a jug made from blue, pharmacist glass. Inside sloshed a molasses-like substance. He crossed the room and went into the kitchen. He came back with a Tupperware box big enough to hold a sandwich. After opening the bottle, he filled the plastic container with some of the dark liquid.

"What's that?"

"Ink." The expression on his face resembled the one he wore just before giving the audience at the Aero the middle finger.

"I have ink."

"Not like this." He finished filling the container. He corked the jug and put the lid on the Tupperware. After handing the plastic box to Chris, he said, "Put that in your printer when you're ready to print the next story you send to *Arbogast*."

"Is it going to make the words look prettier?"

Gunter grunted. He put the jug on a table by the couch. "You must not let the ink touch your hands. When the story is printed, put it directly in the envelope, seal it, and send it off. Even when the ink is on paper, you must not let it get into your skin."

John Henry Francis

Lunch stank. The people from Punting Press were hippies disguised as executives. They came to the meeting dressed in jeans and cheap, K-Mart button-down shirts. The big cheese, Katie Prudent, had sported a flimsy summer dress accenting her form whenever she stood in front of the sun-drenched window.

John Henry Francis looked at himself in the mirror while washing his hands in the restaurant's bathroom. He'd spent twenty minutes that morning getting his hair to spike. Who did these people think they were talking to? His serious-gray Armani suit should have told them who ran the show. His Guess shoes went for five hundred bucks a pair. And they had the nerve to give *him* the shrug?

"Well, Mr. Francis," said Katie, "we'll read the stories and if everyone can come to a positive consensus, we'll take the next step."

Jesus! he thought. What else is there to do? *Space Conflicts*, the 2002 award-winning collection of *Star Wars* rip-offs had been his baby. He wouldn't have set up the meeting if he didn't think the anthology would sell. He wanted to shout at them, "I'm in charge of *Arbogast*, understand? My magazine is in every airport kiosk from here to Buttknuckle, Washington. Has anyone even *heard* of Softshell Press?"

He dried his hands. The hippies caught a cab as soon as they paid the bill. At least they had done that much for him. He hated Japanese food and he hated, even more, leaving midtown. Checking his suit to make sure everything looked straight, his shoulders tugging tight to accentuate work he'd done that morning at the gym, he blew his reflection a smooch and strutted out.

A stack of manuscripts waited on his desk. When he started at *Arbogast*, there had been a team of readers. Once he got the position of editor, he puckered up and kissed the publisher's ass by suggesting the company save money and let the assistants go. "I know what sells," he assured his bosses.

Their interest in profit trumped their taste in literature.

John Henry Francis took his coat off and folded it over a green, vinyl chair in the corner of his office. He sat at his desk and got to work. The first envelope he opened contained a space opera from somebody in Nebraska. Giving it a courteous half page skim, he decided no such thing as a writer from Nebraska existed. The hayseed who had scribbled the tripe hadn't even included a self-addressed stamped envelope. He tossed the whole thing into a round, industrial garbage can.

The next submission: A werewolf yarn written by someone from Boston. The writing stank but the story broke no rules. "I like it," he said. He hadn't read much of it, just enough to know it mimicked what *Arbogast* published since he'd become editor.

He prepared three envelopes with rejection memos, each going out to various states in the middle of the country. "Why don't you guys just stick to farming and working in factories?"

Then he saw a familiar return address. "When is this loser going to get the message?"

Chris Clark. Some artsy-fartsy writer who lived in Los Angeles. Normally, John Henry didn't mind reading anything from the west coast, as long as it adhered to the standards of the magazine. But this Clark guy, he blended genres and did things nobody who consumed horror or science fiction had seen before.

John Henry had read letters sent to *Weird Tales* back when they made the mistake of printing stories by H.P. Lovecraft. The subscribers hated them. They considered them the equivalent of a fat kid whose parents had enough money and gall to send their little tugboat to a finishing school. Certain things just didn't *belong* in the mainstream.

Chris Clark presented a shining example. The pompous jerk probably referred to his scribbling as post-modernism, or some other pompous term the sandal wearing flakes at universities called their radical ramblings in effort to justify their refusal

to be normal. The last time he'd gotten one of Clark's submissions he threw it away without even looking at it.

Feeling charitable, John Henry told himself his conscience would reward him if he gave Chris Clark the same consideration he gave all the arrogant turds who tried new things. He opened the envelop and pulled out the contents. It contained the usual cover letter, detailing Clark's worthless publication credits. Who had ever even heard of *The Magnolia Review*? Some college rag you found on campuses and one or two bookstores that stocked literary journals to silence anyone who bashed them for selling dependable Lee Child and Stephen King novels.

He set the cover letter aside and began reading the story, "Ink and Mirrors." More attempts to be clever in a world that didn't pay a penny for original ideas. John Henry let his eyes scan the first few paragraphs. When he felt he'd read enough, he reached for the pile of preprinted rejection letters.

Then he stopped.

For some reason, whatever

he'd read, it caused a reaction similar to that of tearing down the first hill of the Cyclone, over at Coney Island. He wanted to finish it. As he read on, he recognized the writing as stream-of-conscious. In his mind, he calculated how someone would market it— "It's like Henry Miller meets Harlan Ellison. All the furious attitude of the id, right there on the page."

He shook his head. "What the hell am I talking about?" Publishing it would scar *Arbogast's* reputation. Once more, he tried to put a rejection letter in the self-addressed stamped envelope.

Something stopped him. *I've got to read it all.* Blood rushed through his body, like a twelve-year-old boy finding a stash of *Playboy* magazines in his father's work shed. His heart beat faster. Putting the story in front of his face again, he lost himself in the words, caressed the ink on the page with his fingertips.

The prose looped together like music, like a Charlie Parker solo, flying crazy in and around a melody in a way that should not have worked. Like Dali meets Picasso. James Joyce meets William Burroughs. Nonsense. Beautiful.

"Chris Clark," he said when he finished, "congratulations." He put the story in the acceptance basket on a small table next to his desk. His body continued to tingle with excitement, like the first time a girl had put her hands in his lap. He ignored the sensation and reached for the next submission.

It had been sent from Dubuque, Iowa. Normally, he would have grabbed the SASE, stuffed it with a rejection slip, and moved on until he found a story from one of the coasts. Instead, he took the manuscript out and read it.

Nothing more than a vampire tale set in Chicago. *Maybe I'm learning a lesson.* A thousand words into the story, he noticed the light hitting the page flickered. Craning his head to see if the fluorescent overhead needed to be replaced, he saw the long tubes pulsating blue and white.

"What the hell?"

He cleared the envelopes out of the way and stepped

onto his car-sized, mahogany desk. His Guess shoes failed to grasp the slick surface. He worked to get a footing and reached for the housing on the light and tapped it. Sprinkles, like tiny stars, floated down each time he hit the lamp.

Perhaps I'm having a panic attack. His mother had had them when she went through menopause. She compared it to stumbling into pockets of insanity. He jumped off the desk.

"Just keep reading," he said. He picked the vampire story back up and forced himself to focus on the words. It worked until the sentences melted and bled together. When he held the page away to look at it from a distance, it became an inkblot test, reminding him of all the shrinks his mother took him to throughout his childhood to prove him a genius. She could never find a doctor who would diagnose her son as anything beyond ordinary.

His heart thundered like a drum beaten by a maniac. The far wall of the office bubbled like boiling liquid. "Someone slipped me something at the restaurant," he said. "Damn hippies!" He struggled for the door. The floor waved like an ocean. Air whipped like a violent wind in and out of his ears. He forgot why he'd crossed the room.

Then, for just a second, he forgot *who he was.*

"Oh, dear Jesus," he said. *The police. I'll call the police.* I'll have an ambulance take me to the hospital. They *have* to have something there that will make this go away. He grabbed the phone and put it to his ear. The dial tone wailed like a bomb siren. The cord twisted and turned. A snake, crawling up his arm to strangle him. He threw the receiver at the desk.

The walls closed in, threatened to squish him. Natural light blasted through the window. The only escape, he realized.

Climbing onto his desk once more, John Henry took three steps and launched himself through the cheap glass his cheap bosses had installed to save on air-conditioning. He flew over Madison Avenue and tumbled to the Earth, trying to grab onto ladders and ledges his mind convinced him existed before his entire body spread across the concrete like a glob of jelly.

Gunter Fry

Two rows of his bookshelves were filled with contributor

copies he had received from *Arbogast* and other fantasy magazines over the years. Perfect spines. Most of them had never been opened. He admired them every day just after he finished writing his mandatory two-thousand words. Those stories had built his career.

The jug of ink still sat on his writing desk. He remembered picking it up in Thailand. He'd been an officer in the war. His job: Dispatch troops into the jungle to ward off the Viet Cong. Then, he and the other officers would take a helicopter into Saigon or Malaysia or Thailand. They'd trade cigarettes for whores and consume any drug or alcohol they could find.

Outside a temple in Bangkok, he met a homeless man who claimed to be from Siberia. He spoke perfect English. Gunter told him he wrote stories and the man traded him the ink for a pack of unfiltered Camels.

He didn't believe him at first. Two years after returning to the states, a brutal period in his life when nobody would publish his work, he tried it. Every manuscript he sent out got accepted after that, including his first novel. Once his name had been established,

he no longer needed the ink.

These things ran through his mind as Chris Clark showed up, grinning. Gunter had never seen the kid smile.

"Look at this." Chris held up a large, yellow envelope with the *Arbogast* insignia on the return address. He opened it and pulled out the contract with a check for three hundred dollars stapled to it.

"Congratulations, kid." Gunter let him inside his house. "Guess this calls for a toast."

They climbed the narrow staircase leading to the second floor. At the far end of the hallway, a screen door led to a balcony. From there, they could drink and watch the ocean.

"I assume you used the ink," Gunter said after they sipped from their glasses.

"I'll give you one of the contributor copies when it gets printed."

Gunter almost choked. He waved his hand before he could speak. "Listen, kid," he said, "never read anything that got published because you used the ink."

Chris frowned.

"I know you want to see your story, all laid out professionally." He set his glass down. "The thing is, the ink is only half the magic. Combined with the words, the story itself becomes a drug."

Chris shook his head. "That's absurd."

"Anyone who reads your story now will go mad." He paused, made sure he had the kid's complete attention. Then he said, "Even you."

Stanley Rutgers is a psychologist from Simi Valley. His work has appeared in *Der Graft*, *Killer Tales*, *Angel Therapy*, *Pulp Modern*, *The Stockard Press*, and *The Magnolia Review*.

©
Story: Stanley Rutgers
Art: Brad Foster

Artist Bios

Darren Auck ia a Cartoonist, Illustrator and Art Director. He started writing and drawing his own comics at six years old and self-published magazines while in high school. After graduating from The Kubert School in 1983, Darren worked for Pacific Comics and DC Comics. He also worked for Marvel Comics for ten years as a Bullpenner, Freelance Writer/ Artist and Art Director. Darren's clients include: Rodale Press, Workman Publishing, New York Life Insurance Co., Nickelodeon, The New York Financial Writers Association, BMW, Janssen Pharmaceuticals, The Rock Band AC/DC and various Trading Card Companies. Darren has served as an instructor at The Kubert School for sixteen years and is currently working on creator owned projects: *Jersey Devil VS Bigfoot*, *My Best Friend Bigfoot*, and *Uncle Samson and Son*.

Theo Ellsworth's newest graphic novel, *Secret Life* is an adaptation of a short story by Jeff VanderMeer, published by Drawn and Quarterly. A solo show of his woodcut fine art is currently on view at Giant Robot in Los Angeles. See more of his work on Instagram @theo_ellsworth_

Brad W. Foster is fascinated by robots, both toy and otherwise, to an almost uncomfortable degree. Beyond that persona quirk, he creates artworks with pen and ink and digital dots. He has been published in over a thousand different places, most of which you have never heard of, but you can find them all listed, and other details of a misspent life at JabberwockyGraphix.com

Allen K(oszowski) is one of the most prolific artists in his field, having published more than 2,500 illustrations for hundreds of genre publications, including *Asimov's, F&SF, Cemetery Dance, Whispers, Fantasy Tales, Weirdbook, Weird Tales, The Horror Show, The Robert Bloch Companion*, and many others. allenk.com

Rick McCollum will be launching a (very) small press within about three or four months, depending upon how fast he can draw! Stay tuned!

Michael Neno has written, drawn and published comics, zines, coloring books and more for 35 years. In addition to designing concert posters and album covers, his freelance work includes penciling, inking, lettering and coloring comic books. His latest project, the YA GN Frank Holster Mysteries, are written and published by Jacques Nyemb, and will be available soon. facebook.com/michael.neno/

The Saturday Evening Post dubbed **Bob Vojtko**, the "working man's cartoonist" because of his union-backed day job and his long-time second career as a gag man. Bob's cartoons have been published in just about every major and minor magazine that runs cartoons. He's contributed or self-published dozens of mini comics since the 1970s. You can find him at home drawing more cartoons or on Facebook.

Independent Fiction Alliance

Writers and Publishers Committed to Free Speech

independentfictionalliance.com